Reunion with Rembrandt

By

Cheryl Blaydon

Reunion with Rembrandt

Copyright © 2024 by Cheryl Blaydon

All rights reserved. No part of this book may be reproduced or transmitted in any form or by any means without written permission of the author.

ISBN 978-1-943424-83-2

LCCN 2024943520

North Country Press
Unity, Maine

Author's Note

The premise of this novel is garnered from the events of March 18, 1990, when thirteen pieces of art were stolen from the Isabella Stewart Gardner Museum.

It has been thirty-four years since the largest art heist in history occurred, and to date none of the stolen work has been recovered.

For Leonard Cohen, and for J, who listened.

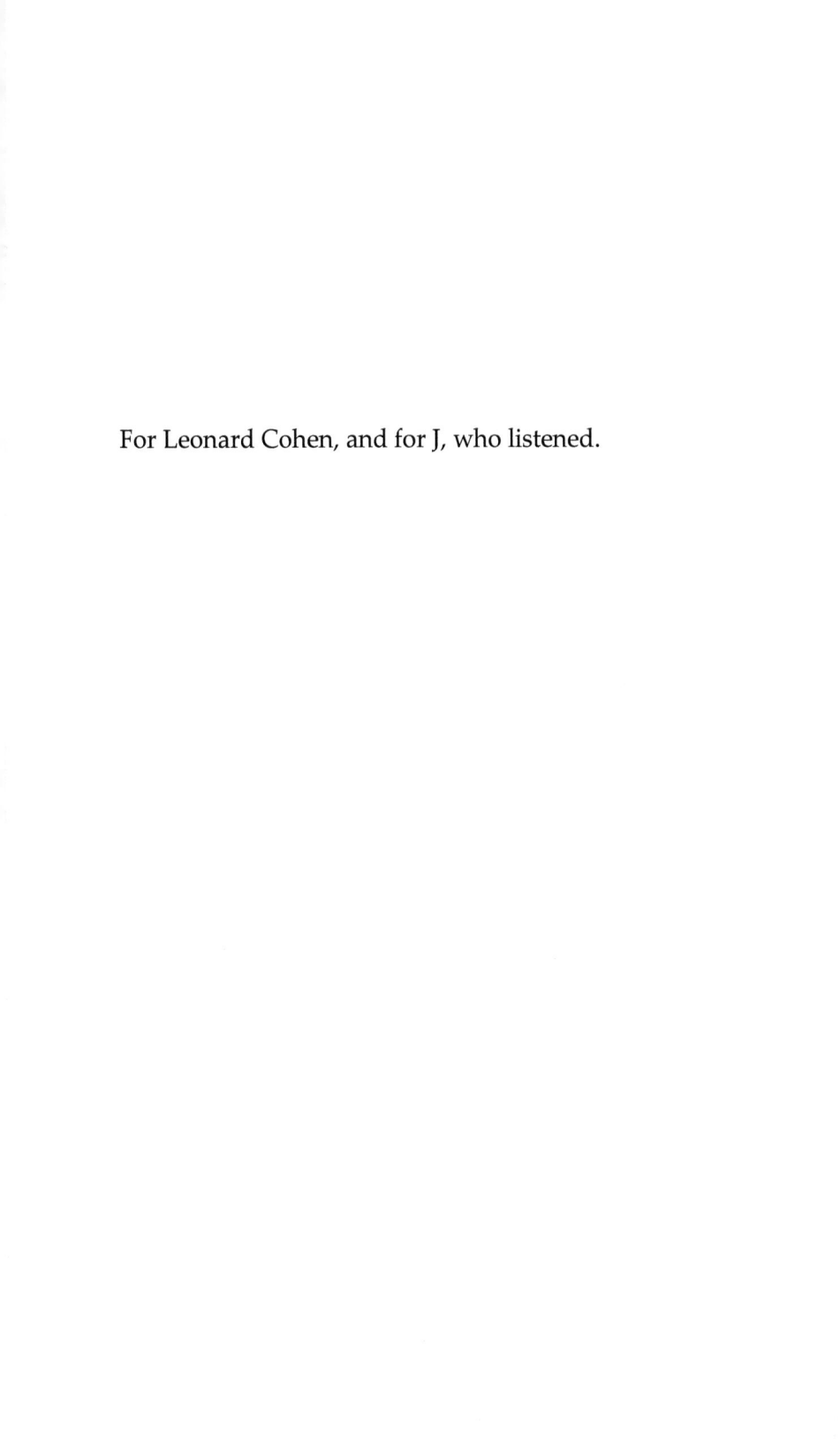

ACKNOWLEDGEMENTS

A big thank you to my small band of early readers: Ruth Alley, Hilary Bartlett, Mary Failing, Pat McKee, and Natalie Sillery, all of whom had at least a segment or two to critique.

And to the late Denise Costello who had the final manuscript and always had my back.

Last but not least, a shout out to author Lara Tupper who helped me find the 'real' beginning while I was still mired in the middle.

Chapter 1

March 18, 2018

Kate Flannagan stood on the platform and squinted. There were no leftover stars. No ribbons of light at the heart of things, only gray pretending to be dawn. It might remain like this all day. Unremarkable. A little like her, she thought as she finally stepped aboard. Faces never before seen softened in welcome. She offered a smile; at least an impression of one. Plumpish lines caught between childhood and maturity. Flannagan lips. Her grandmother Brigid's lips, or so she'd been told. Had this been another day, Kate might have wagered the prospect of a storm brewing or climate concerns: a planet in despair. Mainers loved jawing about weather conditions without much prompting. But today was a morning for self-containment and contemplation. The need to be a silent observer, to slip into her seat before the bull-nosed Downeaster would pull out of Brunswick Station without fanfare and on time. To wait for the dawn light or her mood to change, in no particular order.

Four rows ahead, on the opposite side of the aisle, a man stood up to remove his jacket. Handsome and broad-shouldered, and very tall. He turned slightly, exposing his ruddy complexion. An ad for the Maine woods, she thought and then noticed a slight paunch at his mid-section. An imbibing forest ranger? Or a man who knew his way around a hunting lodge, and good whiskey. Certainly, the opposite of her thrice-married landlord, who had come by just the other day sporting a red plaid shirt, green workpants, and a blue ball cap. He'd said it was time to install a state-of-the-art alarm system. Then he'd bragged about the divorced men he thought she should meet. He'd taken his time with the installation, and his attitude intimated that she needed all the protection she could get.

The gall! He was likeable enough of course, and he'd obviously put in the hours to make her cottage suitable for a rental. Yet, he remained oblivious to the extra creative embellishments she had added in order to make it cozier, more feminine, a real retreat. For him, it was all about those men he'd thought so suitable until her teeth clenched so hard they'd nearly cracked a filling.

Yes, her life was a bit drab at the moment, but who on earth would want to steal what little she had these days. Who could possibly care about trinkets from the guy who'd walked out on her? Or the scribbled-down memories from a marriage that had gone belly up? How about the many thoughts that had been kept in a journal, and then crossed off? Like she'd been, as if twenty-odd years of togetherness meant nothing.

She suddenly bolted upright in her seat; she'd left the house without setting the damned alarm after all. The code numbers were still on the scrap of paper next to the somewhat bulky telephone that had come with the rental—just like the landlord.

Sitting back comfortably, she giggled. A precocious child-like sound.

If something were to happen while she was away for the day, her landlord might be inclined to rethink that list of his. And just maybe he'd find her unworthy of his bowling buddies and even his nephew who hadn't held a job in two years. And leave her alone, until and unless she had need of assistance. How pleasurable, she thought as she felt her toes curl inside the leather boots that she'd paid a fortune for.

But now instead of being in the bosom of her accomplishments, she was on her way to Boston to reignite issues that had been left behind in 2015. Instead of cozying up with an inordinate pile of books, or the hot chocolate made from Mexican cocoa that came wrapped in red as if to indicate the level of heat, she was about to lay a torch to many beloved memories. The calendar said it all; this was the eighteenth of March. A day to ease into rather than crash headlong through the barriers she'd built up these past few years.

She pictured the books that had provided her with paths toward anonymity when she'd first arrived back in Maine. And for some reason, the one that had become a favorite, always on her nightstand for easy reach. And the days left to finish it—for the third time. It had been thumbed-through so often that its spine fell open to page forty-two and the words highlighted with a yellow marker: **jostle, Orient Express, murder.**

But even here, the lines blurred, and like the stupid code, she forgot what would come next when *that* train swept away from Istanbul on its way to Paris. Page fifty might be dicey, or maybe that was fifty-five. And just like the alarm code, there was nothing to be done about things left behind.

Instead, she wandered into the café car, steadying herself as the train took an almost imperceptible curve, and then found a spot to sit and clear her mind of unnecessary distractions.

But without a moment's breath, she ended up pondering what it would be like should a body be found in the sleeping car. Would she become enmeshed in conversation with some agreeable bon vivant. Lovely.

Or not so lovely; she could be stuck with women in pearls and silk dressing gowns with nothing of importance to say. Even worse. Men's faces masked by dark thoughts, all of which was an exhausting exercise for an overcompensating brain.

Still, she left a coffee untouched and returned to her regular seat. The image of the impeccable Inspector Poirot and the woman who may or may not have been in love with him—at least in the film series—floated away along with the passing scenery. It was definitely that kind of day.

And before she knew it, she was enveloped in the sounds of a moving train. A lullaby with different nuances that quickly cradled her into another dreamscape.

Suddenly, her elbow was jostled—or was it jarred—by someone on the run. She looked up and blinked, hard. The Amtrack conductor who bore no resemblance to her British hero, had seemed not to notice at all, and she was as back in real time, and the sky had brightened into yet another shade of gray.

The day was quickly becoming a grisaille painting, she thought, which in turn reminded her of one in the museum. A thought that led to what might be waiting for her when she arrived. Resolve would be nice. But without a doubt, the image of what she'd once been: happily married. And then…what?

Kate moved closer to the window in order to observe the sky. It was definitely still bleak but with a small promise of something she couldn't name. Like her mood. This self-imposed torture to set things right if only in her own mind, and all she could do was watch as the train passed by the stands of trees that lined the tracks and appeared huddled in private conversation. They bore the same tonality of the sky: dull and drab, sad really. Sadder still, she thought, as she realized the pattern, as if the scenery had been choreographed for a moving audience. Trees. Clearings: treeless spaces that exposed the backsides of other peoples' lives.

She cupped her eyes to the glass, suddenly a voyeur witnessing the unexpected. One community after another dusted daily by noise and debris as the train neared the outskirts of

Boston. Would there be a sense of sadness over trips not taken, she wondered. Dormant thoughts brought to life with each new rattle of walls and tilting portraits, or dishes clinking and about to topple within a cupboard. Intimacies that would always be suspended in time even as the train was forced to a specific timetable.

Would her own stories be able to stand up to even the most innocent scrutiny, she wondered as the train pushed forward into the gloom. Would they bear up under memories of things once true and glamorous or at least very amorous. A lifestyle brought to fruition with Angus.

After all, Boston was a far cry from Hull Island, Maine.

But no one would know *their* story unless she chose to divulge what she had believed to be the truth. And then turned out to be a lie.

Stories, other peoples' or her own, and what of the Flannagans of old? She had hardly expected the day to begin this way and now she couldn't seem to find the period at the end — there were too many characters: her father and his youthful struggles and now a brain aged prematurely due to early onset Alzheimer's; a grandmother she mourned the loss of without ever having known the warmth of her arms or what kindness she had to impart. A painting that had disappeared before Kate could know more of its existence.

She considered her father's condition, all the things he no longer remembered; his mood swings and intermittent bouts of clarity; the continual slipping away that the doctor had warned of. How long before he wouldn't remember his mother Brigid or why there was a painting of her out there somewhere. How long before he slipped behind a curtain of gray with no hope of seeing the sun. A day like today, she thought as her own mood switched like a train changing tracks when all along her only intention had been to revisit the scene of the crime: the Gardner's losses, and the crime perpetrated on her heart.

And now, having sworn against returning as long as Angus remained in the city, it seemed as if she'd been mentally picking out her battle gear before the train had even stopped.

She sat back in her seat, her emotions flitting hither and yon like old Irish tales. Boston was but a stone's throw away: the museum was hallowed ground filled with youthful memories; art and antiquities so deeply embedded in her psyche, that they would need to be excavated without thought of the pain that would follow. Otherwise, she might never reach the root cause of her present situation: divorced before fifty.

It was far too late to turn her back on the hours and hours with Angus in those very galleries, both of them exploring art and each other. What if he'd never really loved her; that she was destined to become a cliché, she thought as she turned her face toward the opposite side of the track to find the horizon. She had been taught to do that when she'd been at the helm of the *Mary-Kate*, a way of righting herself to ward off nausea.

Tears began to spring up while at the same time she could feel the train easing into Boston's North Station. And then all she could hear was the sound of pent-up doubts beating louder than her heart ever had.

The other passengers stood and she followed suit. But now the body framed in the oversized window was that of a woman in mourning about to walk under a cloud that had nothing to do with the weather or her shrouded appearance. Both of which would have been an affront to the streets gayly greened from St. Paddy's the day before.

All the sounds vying for attention: a rustle of material, a snap of a newspaper, a bump of a bag on the floor. Conversations whispered while Kate hung back and waited for the scene to unfold. For the casual energy to coalesce as the passengers departed: women walking arm in arm, couples holding hands, a college-aged girl shouldering a large backpack. The way she had done eons ago.

Kate wondered where she would fit in and how someone might perceive her movements when she finally walked off the train. Would they find her interesting or even a little bit mysterious, she wondered as the tall stranger in the seat ahead finally stood to put his jacket back on. It seemed he had pulled a jaunty cap from a pocket because he now had the distinguished air of some estate manager in jolly old, like Edgar come to life from the pages of an old forgotten novel.

He turned and tipped it her way, as if he'd been expecting to be noticed, but she quickly realized he was looking at the woman who'd been seated a few rows behind. A handsome woman in a smart raincoat. Wearing a proper smile.

He smiled back and then blushed, like a girl.

Bless his heart, Kate thought as he strode purposefully toward the innerworkings of the station. Would he stop at some point and wait—in case that woman in the raincoat followed. And what of the others, she wondered. The ones with their umbrellas and phones at the ready. What would make their day better? Were they headed to nearby shops, or maybe a brunch date at a trendy hotel. Or perhaps someone was outside already hailing a cab to the Gardner as she was about to do—but certainly not for the same reason. Not on the eighteenth of March anyway.

Today was the legal date of her divorce, which no one would be bothered about. No one seemed to pay attention to her at all, she realized as in the case of the man with the cap. And even though today Isabella's visionary palace would be throbbing with the memories of the largest art heist in history, no one could discern that she had more recently been robbed.

Because that was what betrayal felt like.

And unlike the enormity of the Gardner's financial loss, who would bother with the plight of a woman shocked into indecision when millions of dollars' worth of art remained at stake? Maybe it was good to be unremarkable. Maybe she'd dissolve within the pillars of history and accomplish more than she'd set out to do.

Art was meant to bring joy and thoughtfulness. And to be honest, she needed both today. And without fuss if possible. Otherwise, she might cry, which even as a child had been too embarrassing to bear, especially when she'd been out lobster fishing with her father and she was the only girl on the docks.

She thought of him again just as she was about to get out of the cab. He hated fuss too, and she had done just that when he'd shown her the photo of her grandmother in a glamorous pose.

Kate wondered if in his diminished capacity, he might have given the Flannagan painting away. Or tossed it out, as if it were part of the trash. She had to keep reminding herself that empathy was needed now more than ever: this man had loved her and raised her and taught her to fish as well as any man. And now he'd be hard-pressed to remember the hours of fun and pride. He was embarking on a new journey, one that would become almost too painful to watch, she thought just as the cab pulled up in front of the museum. She looked about at the streets, the hustle and bustle of more anonymity and considered what difference it would have made if she delayed this trip to Boston for the sake of her dad, to have another go at Brigid's disappearance from their lives. But she really couldn't, could she. The eighteenth was not a date to be trifled with, not since her divorce anyway.

The train ride down from Maine was the final step into her new reality. This date and the impact on her life without Angus. This date that signaled so many losses no matter how many Irish prayers had been sent up. And the significance in the fact that two major works of art had escaped the robbers' blade while decades ago, the eighteenth of March had been churned into chaos.

Chapter 2

It had been three years and a day spent building walls to support her fragile ego before Kate felt secure enough to seek out the remnants of her former life. The *Globe,* which she had continued to follow, still offered a nod to new boutiques, and restaurants, and reviews of food she had yet to experience. The Charles River unspooled in the same manner along the historic Esplanade. And artwork by renowned painters who had haunted her thoughts in the previous months, had remained on view inside the museum. All of this and more, without shouting from the rooftops that this was the building where she had fallen in love. The place where she had scattered her growing pains like seeds meant to be nurtured and take root in the protection of the museum greenhouse.

Kate plucked up her Irish fortitude as she pushed open the museum door, taking for granted that no one would notice that she was shaky-legged. A puppet-on-a-string—a divorcee without a cause. Oddly tugged between relief and a strange hum in her ears, as if she were listening through cotton. The s in Angus's name stretched out like a hiss.

Humming ensued; the entryway was already abuzz. She spotted the two women from the train who were still arm-in-arm, a sisterhood by birth or by friendship, a happy scene that made her wish for her friend Maggie's companionship.

But Kate didn't wave. And those women were quickly swallowed into a group waiting on a guided tour. She supposed she should be grateful that there seemed to be no one around this morning who might recognize the way she had changed, and not all for the better.

It was an odd conundrum: to be seen and recognized or to go unnoticed to save the embarrassment of being seen as pathetic. A scorned woman in some beloved novel. Had she been a little crazy to think she could simply bask in the scent of expensive perfume the way she used to. Because against all odds, she had dabbed on the Chanel that she'd nearly emptied into the sink the night before.

Angus used to bask; she remembered that all right. But what of other men, like those two who just happened to be rushing past from the opposite direction. Their suits cut a path of importance, but their eyes turned away, as though they'd already decided how insignificant she'd become.

It was still difficult to grasp what had happened. The fact that she was no longer part of a couple but still felt as though she were. Bound together for eternity, they used to say. How sick was that, she thought as she suddenly recalled a friend of her mother's, a woman whose attitude had turned other relationships sour.

Kate couldn't afford souring at this stage in her life. And she couldn't afford being sad or invisible either. A woman, who out of desperation, habitually talked to herself. And would thereby be ignored altogether.

Her steps quickened, and so did her pulse, and in that rush of movement she realized the real mistake: three years had not been long enough after all. The perfume that she had dared to wear began to taunt her, as if there was a trail of Chanel, like breadcrumbs, that led from the train to the Gardner doorstep. But this time Angus wasn't following.

He'd understood its power. Had loved the smell of it on her body, and the way the scent floated over the bedsheets afterward. The perfume had become the gift that kept on giving.

But what of today, when the scent began to infiltrate the many corridors of the museum. She sensed her face reddening with the memory: the seductiveness of the scent and the way it used to become entangled within the maze of early morning sex. Or linger in the late afternoons when he played hooky from work. She had never asked him if it followed him into his office afterward.

And he'd made certain that a supply was always at her fingertips. She had thought his generosity was endearing and as delicious as his post-coital attention. She felt a dizzying sensation; her body was heating up of its own volition. And then she gasped. Her hand flew to the warmth of her face—it's *him*. She stopped dead in her tracks.

From the back, he looked like Angus. She sped up, closing the gap until she realized his gait was very different. As was the way his arms fell to his sides. And then whoever *he* was, turned to his right and disappeared into another tour group. She forced herself to keep going, as if nothing had happened even though her emotions were now all over the place.

Would it ever be easier, she wondered and then she thought of the mystery novel and the train and for some reason, evidence. A crime of passion, as if the heady scent she loved so much had been sucked into the walls of the museum. There had been many afternoon rendezvous when he was supposed to be working. Would that scent still be there to be used against her for being so stupid.

How easy it was to picture the perfume as patterns; edges and forms that would have been exuded onto the walls by her body whenever Agnus was around. Or to imagine gloved hands and blue booties and a spray bottle pointed at those same walls, knowing that leftover patterns would glow in the dark, like on TV. And she'd be nailed for loving him too much.

She smiled then, and her breathing normalized in a way it hadn't since she'd left the train. And then she lifted her hand to fix her hair and thick floral notes flew from her wrist and assaulted her nose and stirred her quiet parts. As if she had only just wakened from the massive bed that he had once negotiated into their bedroom after they had finally tied the knot.

It was more difficult to imagine that mattress (she presumed he'd kept it) had acquired a new inhabitant.

She had been foolish to think she could bypass the way they had loved and the magnitude of that love, especially while wearing the Chanel. *You should have realized that coming back here would be as dicey as a literary train ride.* Images of the way they had once been hovered in the air, and those scenes were all fighting for attention.

But how would she ever find relief except perhaps in another bed at another time and maybe a new location. She wasn't getting any younger after all. Standing here, she thought of her new friend Maggie, and the way she so easily dispensed encouragement. And right at this moment, Maggie would insist that Kate put on a game face and continue on. What were friends for, after all.

Kate lifted her shoulders and straightened her spine. But what about her deer-in-the-headlight expression, she thought—caught between all those rocks and hard places. As if all those morning affirmations pasted on her bathroom mirror had been a ridiculous waste of time. Just that very morning, she had begged the universe, literally cried out for her mother as she had right after Mary died. She had been a great believer in signs. She was a Libra. Kate was a Scorpio and never read those daily horoscopes.

She felt the tears threaten; she missed her mother terribly. The diminutive Mary Flannagan was a force to be reckoned with and she would have been the first to point out that the man whom Kate had fallen for and had beckoned to from beneath her fringed eyelashes in this very museum, hadn't been worth her time after all.

But he had been worth it—back then at least, she thought and then she spotted a man wearing the worst fitting jeans ever. *He should have kept it in his pants*—a favorite of her mother's, a perfect sign. Mary had to have been listening, right?

Verbal incontinence was at one time one of her mother's attempts at humor, though not always successful. Especially when it came to cheaters.

Her mother had spent very precise moments debating the cheating husbands of Hull Island, not only with her own husband (who hadn't dared), but with St. Patrick: *to lighten the case load of Father Sheen,* or so she'd said. And she would have been appalled by Angus's behavior. *The balls on the man!* Kate shot a glance heavenward. "Right on, Mum."

But looking back on her childhood, Kate again remembered the times she'd listened by the rickety screen door as she made small rock cairns for her own amusement. Or when she'd been sitting beneath the chipped kitchen window with her paint sticks, trying to draw the shape of the boats sailing toward the horizon.

Her mother's words were carted from the house on the back of her father's. Their conversations like building drumrolls as they poured out on the aroma of freshly baked pies. Much of what they'd said could easily have been used for Angus now. Just as it was obvious that many of her mother's past indictments would be very suitable for 2018.

The wife of a lobsterman, Mary was outspoken and then contrite. She had a profound fear of the sea and the sound of the demented wind that could be heard rattling the windows in the dead of night.

Fortunately, she never forgot that the same dark and sometimes treacherous water also nurtured their livelihood.

Her upbringing had made her fearful of sin as well (though her diatribes to the parish priest rarely reflected that). And had she lived to see Kate's signature on those divorce papers, her strongest fear would have been for her daughter's very soul.

And now, her mother, from her 'elevated' vantage point—would know that Kate had been made a fool. And that was something far more brutal to bear.

Kate felt a knot of painful circumstances pushing against her stomach: the thought of her mum's pies; the cruelty of a sudden hunger for tasty grains (she'd skipped breakfast); the desire to fit back into her jeans without moving the button. And then there was the local bakery that she would pass on her way home from the train.

But Maggie's instructions were clear: *just remember, this is only another form of therapy, a simple walk down memory lane, Kate, not the last Crusade!*

When she reached the landing, Kate stopped with such urgency she nearly toppled over. She whipped out her phone and texted Maggie: **help!**

She waited, and then checked the time. It was too late. Maggie was already headed for the Farnsworth Museum in Rockland. Floors and floors of fine art, most of it very unlike the art of the Gardner.

But today was also when Maggie would be meeting someone new, Kate thought. A man who professed to share an interest in New England artists. But who could really know if he was legit until it might be too late.

She had cautioned Maggie to no avail just the day before, had even tried to warn her off the whole online dating thing. Maggie had smiled as always, explained her motives, and presumed that Kate understood. But she hadn't. Other than the idea that Maggie, a community-minded computer nerd, would find it difficult to meet anyone while she was doing research on the effects of PFAS. She spent countless hours at the Curtis Library in Brunswick sifting through Maine and New Hampshire research and news articles, which was hardly conducive to any romance at all.

They had built a strong bond in a short period of time, maybe Kate's only real friend since she'd never had time to make that type of friend while married to Angus. And maybe that was typical of many close marriages. But who knew, maybe it had been Kate's own fault.

It was suddenly as if her thoughts were running amuck, which reaffirmed the fact that she probably shouldn't have come back here today. Even the elevens between her brows seemed to deepen, to dig in as if arranging a permanent home. She was stressing and needed to call Maggie and invite her over for drinks later on. Who better than Maggie to help, Kate thought as she pinched the bridge of her nose. She tucked her phone back into the purse slung crosswise on her chest, and then swept her fingers upward, like in the makeup tutorial, careful not to push too hard. She pictured Maggie's flawless skin and swiped upward one more time before heading down to the Cloister.

And when she finally reached the threshold to what she considered the finest gallery in the museum, there was a buzz against her hip. Her tiny purse had carried the weight of Angus's indiscretion, all her blame and his hope for a realignment, as if he could draw a new map on their relationship. And this gallery was the one place that had been truly theirs outside of their bedroom.

She was hardly ready to answer the phone or to enter the gallery for that matter. Even with a three-year hiatus, this would always be the place where love and hate and all the in-betweens would surge like a disabused tsunami.

The Cloister, with all the best memories of Spain and tapas and bold red wines. A country that was at one time synonymous with her love for Angus. He was still hail and hardy, but his presence, his voice and the promises he'd made, were now only in her mind. Fresh and very raw.

The Cloister had been the precursor to a rich affinity with fine art. The room where she'd met Angus for the first time. Kate had called their meeting a seductive road to her maturity. Maggie had called it a 'cute-meet'. In fact, they might both be right, as if there was a true intersection between love and art. A road that Kate had hoped to walk forever.

And even after the trips were no longer viable and she had headed away from Boston, she'd kept up with the music of Spain. Had carved up the headiness of those times spent in a country that managed to come to life here in the Cloister.

This had to have been part of Isabella's grand plan, for who else could have given the public what they hadn't known they needed. Treasures found abroad were on view throughout the entire museum. The Cloister adjoined the living collection of art…the flowers and plants that grew amongst the solid pillars and pots that looked as if they'd been there for centuries as well. It was a Venetian-style courtyard, a world unto itself and protected by a clear domed canopy. The Spanish Cloister and its Italian neighbor, connected by a low wall.

And for Kate, John Singer Sargent's masterful painting waiting at the end of the gallery. She only had to summon her nerve. To remember the blessings that it bestowed and without the painter's ever having planned it that way. Kate's hands could still feel the brushes she had used while at Boston College; the excitement of a splash of color screaming across a canvas or a dollop of spilled paint on her clothes, as if it was solid proof that she was an artist even though it was too soon for a degree.

But Sargent's painting had been judiciously housed in what appeared to be its own sanctuary. The music she had come to love: guitars and castanets and pounding heels. Shouts of *ole* that were a song unto themselves.

It was all piped in of course, but that didn't make it any less real. And not long after moving to Boston, the Cloister had become Kate's first sacred place. And once-upon-a-time, her heart's true home. But now what? Where could she house her heart in a way that felt safe after what had happened to the gist of her life.

Her psyche had been damaged, but not irreparably. Her figure had changed, but hopefully not forever. She knew she had to let him go. And she had to let go of the repetitive image of the woman (Kate refused to say her name) who had moved in and taken over. And without so much as a thank you note.

Standing here today, it was easy for Kate to look back at the day that she'd rushed back to Maine, leaving Angus and his shiny new prize to their own messy sorting. Then, in a simple and unscripted way, Kate found herself tangled in different sheets.

New pillows had become soaked from the reservoir of tears that never seemed to empty. And then one day, they dried up. At least long enough to get dressed and make a plan.

Covering the circles with makeup had become doable, but the dreamer in her had fervently wished for something to soften the ragged edges of hurt. An airbrush to blur the lines on the disagreeable. Sadly, there was nothing available at any make-up counter that would remove the bitterness that lingered on her tongue with every mention of Angus's name.

Did she hate him, she wondered for the umpteenth time, or just what he'd done? And would it make a difference to her future. Her only consolation, and it was small in the grand scheme of things, was that her mother hadn't lived to bear witness to what Angus's infidelity had caused Kate to become—a bitch—personified. A woman who cursed like those long-ago Flannagans. And then she'd left him and the rest of Boston behind.

"There's more to it than that!" Kate's voice, suddenly reedlike, spilled out as she was reminded of the road taken. The one that had led to such an ungainly downfall.

It all began at the end of her last summer in high school. She'd walked the halls and stairways and the grounds of their three-tiered house. Through tears, she'd watched the *MaryKate*—skating on the tides—its bow tightly tethered to a bright orange mooring ball. Blinded by those same tears, she'd headed south, having chosen Boston over an in-state college.

But there was another memory too. Her father distraught, but her mother finally mollified into a peaceful coexistence with St. Patrick and his cohorts—Kate had chosen a new path away from the sea.

But this was now, and she had gone back to Hull Island like a refugee without a true plan and feeling as though she were carrying the weight of the world. A troubled world no less, and one far more important than Kate's issues. Her problems were like a minor scuffle against a planet poised for disaster. Did she dare soil what had been really fine, she wondered as she took in her surroundings: the glazed tiles and objects of worth, the dialogs she silently held with the stone cutter responsible for the weighty sarcophagus.

Or the tile maker who'd done a one-of-a-kind piece that rested in the niche near the wall. The Cloister as a whole. Would it continue to be a safe harbor, with or without Angus.

As if answering her thoughts, a curse emerged from the other side of the wall. Nothing like those of her own of late. But going up on her toes, she peeked over, only to see a museum employee taking off his heavy gloves to inspect his hand. It was red, but without a spot of blood, so she took a chance and cleared her throat and said, "Excuse me." He turned around, and gave her a sheepish smile and said, "I didn't know anyone was there."

"I didn't hear a thing," she lied. "But are you by any chance getting ready for Isabella's birthday celebration?"

"I will be in a minute, but see up there—". He raised himself from a kneeling position, still holding his hand, his face gleaming with sweat. "We have to repair those few railings first. Then a touch of paint and we're done." Kate followed his left arm as it pointed upward to the man who was crouched inside one of the balconies.

Kate was suddenly beside herself. She pictured Isabella. Perhaps dressed in gauzy white, maybe on holiday in Venice. Standing in an Italian *sala* overlooking one of the canals. Could it be that was where she'd gotten the idea for the peek-a-boo balconies for the Gardner.

"I can't wait!" Kate said as if this gardener held that same image.

This time she really envisioned a happier train ride back to Boston in April. "I love the nasturtiums!

"We're almost ready!" To emphasize this, he pointed at Kate and then gave a thumbs up to his partner who was wielding the paintbrush. The man waved back, and Kate said, "I'll leave you be."

But her mind had already fast-forwarded to the nasturtiums. They were cultivated over many months before they were pruned to perfection. When ready, they'd be formed into long streamers that would be hung from all the balconies in celebration of Isabella's birthday. And in the only shade of orange that Kate tolerated anymore.

Orange—an inescapable agent—a color that had become reminiscent of childhood. And later, the unrepentant hue that had managed to snag her attention the first time she walked into the Cloister.

That was the day she had first noticed the pigments used in John Singer Sargent's masterful painting. The day she realized that he had defined with paint what words—even her own—failed to accomplish.

No one on the planet would understand how over the years, *El Jaleo* had turned into a top-to-bottom summary of what had once ailed her and what had given her hope. It was more than a story that she had concocted solely for entertainment.

Not only had Sargent's work tied her to Angus out of their mutual love for his skill, but this strong painting represented a time piece that chimed the exact moment when she'd had to admit that hers was a pitiful talent. The day she had to bid goodbye to Boston College and a future that might have been.

Kate's temperature suddenly rose—totally out of context—a flush of red on her neck that couldn't be stopped. Heat that she had been informed was just another admonition of a body about to turn fifty. Even without a mirror, she understood where the patches of red had started to form and the track to her forehead. Such an embarrassment she thought though no one else was there to notice. Embarrassing or not, there was nothing she or anyone could do about them.

And then, as if lit from within, the scent of Chanel swelled against the flush and stifled the air around her like some kind of punishment for past behavior. Like the heat dripping from the walls upstairs...not forensic this time, but evidence of how truly they had lived in their love back then.

When he'd been the man with a raw-boned energy who'd instigated a future together—a grown-up life. And she had been a mere eighteen, formed for the most part by Hull Island's working waterfront. And literally off the boat before boarding the train to Boston for the first time.

Chapter 3

Kate waited a few moments for the heat to recede and then mentally reclaimed that girl—the one without all this cumbersome emotional baggage. The teenager who'd gone from a student to a believer in the power of art—the lives it touched, and the minds it could change.

Back then, she had drunk it all in the way others used alcohol, and lived off the high of imagined fame and fortune. The downside was that no potion could provide those outcomes or strengthen her skills.

But no matter how hard she struggled at BC or what was happening with Angus during those first two years, the Cloister had opened its arms on her greedy wants. It had embraced the girl with floral prints and madras checks and flaring bell-bottoms.

Later, this very same space had consumed the young woman who could pull all-nighters and still be dewy faced in the morning. Who'd navigated the bustling traffic, city lights, and sidewalk cafes. And perused the museum at every turn with the lover who took her breath away. A time when their conjoined heat might easily short circuit any electrical grid.

And after all of that, living (in sin) with Angus without bothering to phone home because how could her parents possibly understand the unrelenting agonies of her first real love.

But time had marched on; she was nearly middle-aged (depending on which statistics table she checked), and hidden beneath *faux* pashmina of all things. Why spend tons on the real thing just to mask the thickness of her waist. And if she were lucky, the bit around her hips.

Today's outfit, minus the chunky turquoise necklace, would have been more suitable for the Irish wakes her mother once insisted she attend. Kate's emphasis on dark clothing had become a ruse meant to trick herself into believing otherwise.

In reality, clothing of any sort would do nothing to detract from the number of pounds that had accumulated during the empty hours as she tried to reconfigure her steps without Angus. It was time to own it, she thought; she had allowed herself to be caught up by a sense of failure. And without a doubt, there was no color to paint that would describe such a feeling.

Being blindsided was also not an excuse and there was no way to paint that away either. No color to choose from on any of her charts. And no one else to blame. She'd failed to notice the small nuances: the tailored jacket that fit him better than anything else that he owned, and supposedly purchased for a short business trip; the boxer/briefs in colors she wouldn't have dared to buy knowing how he preferred those from his usual store. Even a different haircut...still longish but trimmed with new purpose.

Then it was too late. After that, she had fled to Maine, and he had dragged out what should have been an easy process. Even with his new relationship to consider, he'd obviously used the time as a way to punish her for not taking him back when he first asked.

But a year ago today—perhaps through guilt, or simply that he'd tired of his own game—he'd put her out of her misery and signed the damn papers. And without a preemptory phone call to give her time to catch her breath, they had arrived in a blue binder, and as casually as the morning paper. Proving the male ego was a funny thing indeed.

And of all days—the eighteenth of March—the same date that thirteen highly valued pieces of art and sculpture had been stolen from their galleries on the floors above her,

"Who does something like that?" Kate's words collapsed into the air, but he may as well have requested matching tattoos. The date, deeply embedded in her brain, signaled the type of news that still resonated within the art world, and Boston in particular. But *they* would never know that for her, this date was now synonymous with more endings than beginnings.

And yet, she hadn't been able to rid herself of the Chanel. Oh, she'd been conflicted all right: vilify the giver or glorify a gift made of liquid gold.

As a Flannigan first and foremost, she'd done the math: emotional cost versus financial. It hadn't taken a genius to figure out the answer. The prismed glass stopper was then placed back into its signature bottle. Not with kid gloves, but with a loud and resentful clink. It was the best that she could do. In a simple act of rebellion, she had decided she should wear it today, and look where that had gotten her!

Against all odds, she had allowed herself to be vulnerable again. No one, except Maggie—who walked the walk and offered better advice than anyone—understood: *we're too old to recreate the blossoming of youth, and too young to demand less of what life offers.*

Kate leaned in as if she could harness that wisdom the way she had come to lean on Maggie even though they were the same age. But Maggie had promised to be here the next time, because in her own inimitable way, she'd said, *there will always be a next time!*

Sadly, neither of them could figure out how they could manage that flush of all flushes.

Kate whipped off the shawl again as she pictured the woman at the cash register in the supermarket in Brunswick just the day before. She'd been full of sage advice about home remedies, which she dispensed in front of all the other customers. Kate could still feel the perspiration flowing down her back just thinking of the embarrassment.

And now in the midst of another heat wave, the speakers pulsed to life. They sent familiar notes to seep into the still-empty gallery. Music to awaken a soul and lift a dreary heart right out of its body, or so it felt. She tried to push aside the extra heat and imagine the way a flamenco would appear as sheet music, the bold steps against fine black lines.

These were beloved sounds. They filled her pores, her lungs, and on some deeper level, her cravings. *Get on with it now.*

Before taking up with 'the other woman', Angus used to lean over Kate and kiss her as if to reinforce what had become their mutual love for Spain. Their delight as fingers danced on a guitar. Shared secrets: what they'd seen and done and had lived fully. But it was over. And there was no other choice but to relearn how to love again.

And then, without warning, *El Jaleo* pulled at what was left of her heart strings: free-falling into love, and those days and weeks and even years when she and Angus couldn't keep their hands off each other. And when the lust wore off, how they'd still been solid and whole.

Decades ago on a hot summer day, Kate had stepped off another train, her eyes nearly swollen shut from crying. She had no mind for stands of trees or other peoples' lives as she'd barely been able to imagine what she would find once in Boston, other than a course-load of work that might secure her dreams.

Then she'd met Angus. And everything changed: he'd usurped her professors and schooled her in art as he saw it. And then, he'd schooled her in the intricacies of lovemaking, and initiated her into his world of words.

A supreme storyteller, she hadn't known (or cared) that his negative reviews often made people cringe. Just as long as he refrained from criticizing her own amateur artistic endeavors.

She in turn, had become a safe place for him to fall, which gave her a purpose she'd never expected. And here she was now with nothing left to say. No way to sentence together the way a marriage contract could be severed after being tied with such a secure knot.

Again, she thought of Maggie; grief came in various stages and for differing reasons. Her friend's pain had come from being widowed so young, whereas her own was mostly from feeling that she was far too old to start over. But what of her grandmother, Kate thought; who had befriended her in a time of need. And what of the missing painting, and what she imagined to have been an assault on provincial minds. It was the thirties after all.

Did Brigid have a friend like Maggie to sort and sift through the rubble of a broken heart. Because Brigid Flannagan's heart had to have been broken or her praises would have been sung all over Hull Island. There had been nothing but silence about the woman who shared Kate's DNA, a woman with curls like her own, eyes like hers, lips too, a woman who might have been able to nurture her in a different way than that of her mother. It was as if Brigid had been set adrift, like a skiff in a stormy sea, never to be found again.

Chapter 4

1936

Brigid Flannigan was wrapped in a threadbare sweater two sizes too big. She planted her feet and leaned against the weathered rail that was meant to hold her in place while the tumultuous rage she felt, pushed against it. For a young June day, the mist looked thick as snow and devoured all but the edge of a sail and the high stern of her husband's three-masted 'coaster'. Even to her keen eye, the schooner appeared like a ghost ship, though James was certainly at the helm. The *Lady Dora* was on its way to fill its hold with granite quarried near their home on Hull Island. The glittery stone most likely earmarked for a monument or better still, the steps fronting a courthouse further south. Brigid's rigid shoulders slumped. Saturday she would need to confess, but today she prayed that the sole idea of her discomfort, this waiting for him to disappear beyond a hidden horizon, might portend a new beginning.

James had once again left her in a state so harmful to her mind and body, that she had to shoo Tommy back to his bed without his usual attention. He'd been fussy and whiny and her husband made it clear that she was a silly woman—"no brains at all" he'd shouted. Then he'd slammed doors and pushed his plate toward her for a refill. This little drama had happened at first light. He had an appetite she couldn't quench.

How she hated herself this morning, more so than usual because Tommy had been a witness to her fear. And as soon as

James had left the house, she'd gone outside to the widow's walk. And like all the other times, she wondered if it had been named as such in honor of women like her: fearful and unhappy. Or like her, for women making sure their husbands wouldn't turn back and they could breathe a sigh of relief, until the next time. For Brigid, this watching held a quiet loathing, her eyes keeping him in sight until he was nearly at the end of the lane. In her imagination, the lane led to an escape from this drab existence, when in reality it wound up at the village dock and then splintered off to adjacent buildings that housed parts and supplies. Those places were also hidden today. She knew that fishermen waited inside the small shacks set off the end of a dock to the right of her sightline. On good days, she could see smoke curling up from short stacks, but today any smoke would join the mist and disappear completely.

She had heard the muffled sound of James's boots as they sloshed through the mud left over from yesterday's downpour that had turned edges of new grass to mush. That sound held a certain comfort too, like the brandy sloshing around inside his canvas sack as always. And who knew what might happen on a day like this.

So today she would remain grateful for his disappearance into that fog. And for a little while at least, her days would be peaceful. Even if not righted or exactly to her liking. According to dockside chatter, her husband was already being called 'old man Flannagan' by his crew. Brigid knew that it would be years—though probably not fewer bottles—before he'd match his father's skills at sea. But at forty-two, James had managed to surpass the reputation for meanness that had migrated through earlier generations like a virus without a cure.

Her own parents must have been dimwitted to think he'd make a suitable husband. As if his condition as a young widower with a house that dominated a grassy knoll, needed something brightly wrapped to decorate the parlor and bolster his spirits. They had no way of knowing, because Brigid refused to tell them for fear of reprisal, that her once slim waist and blue eyes set against nearly unmanageable dark auburn curls, had not done the trick. Instead, those once-prized attributes had turned the table and crushed *her* spirits while he'd remained the same. After that, she'd stopped writing to them altogether because the only words that landed on the paper were blameful.

And then, she'd stopped writing in her diary too; it reminded her that it had been their graduation gift. Luckily, she had met Helen Budreau at a charity bazaar and then again at the post office. She'd been rolling her eyes at Luke, the postmaster, who was known for his persnickety ways. Brigid had been intrigued and began to think about putting her thoughts down on paper again. She and Helen might become kindred spirits. They might even have fun together, though Brigid wasn't certain she knew what that meant anymore.

Describing Helen within the simplicity of lined pages might be more of a challenge. She was a willow of a woman, not at all akin to the childbearing figure Brigid had earned during those months before Tommy was born and she'd been too tired to leave the house.

Helen's hair was different in every light; sometimes honey blond and sometimes strawberry blonde. And her eyes might be a true green or possibly hazel, depending on what she was wearing. Though more often than not she would wear her brother's plaid shirts for the fun of it, along with a pair of trousers that made her look very tall. Brigid wasn't certain about how badly Helen wanted a husband but she was more than well versed about everything there was to know about men in general. In fact, from what Brigid could tell, Helen's ambitions seemed primarily centered on the topic.

It was too bad, really, that Brigid had come to hate the man she had agreed to marry in the church that sat on the knoll opposite the Flannagan house. Otherwise, she and Helen might have had easier things to talk about.

Brigid had never told Helen how the *Lady Dora* had come to be named. But she hated that James had glorified his late wife while at the same time disparaging the woman's inability to give him an heir. Even after she had died trying. Brigid prayed for Dora's soul too. She also prayed that she wouldn't become pregnant again.

She walked back inside; Tommy's eyelids were twitching in his sleep, his feathery dark hair shiny from the humidity. His small fingers were curled around his stuffed bear, so she tiptoed to the kitchen and left him to his dreams.

She poured a cup of coffee and went into her own bedroom to bring out her diary and start anew.

Chapter 5

2018

On that fateful day in March of 1990, the Gardner had suffered a theft so large it became a national phenomenon. The range of the stolen art had taken on a life of its own. Raw emotions and a huge financial toll had been left for others to work out.

But for Kate, the crux of the matter was in the leavings. Upstairs in another gallery empty frames had been hung on cheery walls as if waiting for guests habitually late to the party. How did those in charge go about reordering their lives after such an event, Kate wondered. And how could she come back here and compare the loss of one man's love to what those others had been through. In truth, she couldn't, but that didn't make her own loss any less significant. And why was she suddenly thinking of amends.

The newspapers who had crucified the Gardner employees, had placed them under a critical spotlight in the aftermath of an unthinkable debacle. But were they expected to make amends for something so far out of their control. Something that might have prevented the robbery, like a proper alarm system. Or real guards instead of college kids who needed extra cash. A lot of what Kate hadn't known at the time had come to light through documentaries on various anniversaries.

And what of her own amends; her mother was gone. Was there time with her father; she'd denied them their dream of grandparenting and especially a chance for another Flannagan to take the helm. Would he even understand or care, now he was battling the first stages of Alzheimer's.

Time may have run out on making amends to Angus—the way she had denied him the one thing he rarely talked about. But then, guilt could be a powerful foe.

Then she nearly screamed. When had she become so absorbed with a pile of regrets, that she failed to recognize that no matter what, she *was* living that grown-up life! And, she was living it in a way that only she could have designed!

Her first love had been for art. Not Angus. And, just maybe, this was the real lesson she was meant to take away at day's end.

And then, as if to confuse this new clarity, another insistent buzz vibrated against her hip. She grimaced; it was telepathy at play for sure—Angus, texting again. At the same time, the overhead sound system burst into the opening bars of "Malaguena". It pulled her back; drowned out the doubts, the hurts, and left what was needed as it thrummed against her chest. The richest of notes hollowed out the place where those doubts had lived. Where love had once dwelled and perhaps might again—despite any change of heart his texts had previously intimated.

And with her changing thoughts, the musical tempo changed too, only this time, it was a slide-like tension and then release. She swayed as if hearing it all anew even though it was written on her heart. If she was guilty of anything, it was that she'd stuffed down everything that had made her happy. She had acted the way every living creature would, and that act was called self-preservation.

A riff broke through her thoughts; an invitation to move her feet and align herself with the dance. Had she lived in Isabella's time, an invitation to any performance might have come on a silver salver. Especially to the balls held here during the heyday of 1903. Those invitations would have been quiet and tasteful, but as far as Kate was concerned, not nearly as exciting as the experience of this classical refrain. She marveled at the woman who dared to draw outside the lines and wore gold brocade to her own dances. Isabella's demeanor always seemed to be ahead of her time and just different enough from the habits of the other women of Boston society.

While Kate would not be able to emulate Isabella's ways, she did want to shed the extra pounds and along with them, the emotional restrictions that she had placed on herself. Men left all the time; she only had to ask. It was all over the big screen and in many of her own books. If she were to delve into a conversation at a supermarket, she would probably find heartbreak lurking in the breakroom or in the aisles or behind the meat counter. It was called life, and there was still a great deal of it to live...if Kate allowed herself to do so.

Through the years, she had always placed a great deal of emphasis on Isabella's story, as if believing them to be *sympatico*. It had a lot to do with Rembrandt of course; not the gold brocade and tiaras that might have been worn back then.

And because of her own story, Kate had a need to believe that Isabella had been struck by the same feelings when she first came upon *El Jaleo*. It was, not only a true flamenco, but a masterpiece of proportion: the width and height and proximity to the gallery floor; the canvas slightly tilted to give the impression that one could step directly onto the painted stage; the addition of music to enhance and bring it to life.

This was the real party that had been taking place while she had been away. This invitation to partake in the implied noise that rousted an unseen crowd. To delve into the unwavering shadows that appeared attentive to the seated musicians. The orange that needed to be peeled — that spot of color, just so.

And a flame-like orange on the dress of the woman off to the right who could barely contain herself — like Kate, wanting to holler out loud, even now.

And all of this was juxtaposed now with her feelings for Angus and what couldn't be undone, *all because he couldn't keep it in his pants.*

Yet there was no denying a world that Sargent had made real—for her. It was more than a love affair. *El Jaleo*—loosely translated 'the ruckus'—had quite simply, altered her life.

This painting was darkness and light. It screamed and rattled against the cage of her heart. And she dared to hope that she would stand here on another day in the not-too-distant future. To take heart in Sargent's masterpiece the way she used to. And not find hopelessness because of what she'd lost.

There were other paintings of course; those on the second floor—her next stop. Canvases that depicted men who battled with swords and armor. Mothers who swaddled their children in serenity. Paintings covered walls in colors that she could never achieve from tubes of oils with such exactitude. Shades of crimson; golds like ocher and leaf, lemons and delft blues. Even rose and brown madder, which she'd mixed incorrectly.

But if it was serenity she was looking for, it wouldn't be found within *El Jaleo*. The painting still brimmed with tension and emotion, laughter and light. Another reminder of how difficult it had been to live with an art critic.

Had he been here today, he would have skewered her to the spot for attempting to paint this scene with her own words instead of waiting for his to be printed in the *Globe*.

And he could go to hell, she thought.

"This *is* the room where it all began," Kate whispered when she would have preferred to shout. And what of Brigid? What would it have been like to have been under scrutiny, to be in her situation. Had the artist been out for himself, knowing that her beauty would provide the money he would most likely attain when he sold the painting.

Or was theirs a true love, for why else would she have jeopardized her reputation. Yes, Kate thought, Brigid's life had also been altered by art. And obviously by Giacomo Canelli, the artist whose name appeared at the bottom of the photo. Her father, in one of his moments of true clarity, called it *Summer Dreams*, which she thought was a euphemism but could not explain why.

Unlike the Gardner's loss, the loss of that painting bore no financial burden. But it mattered a great deal to Kate that she and Brigid were genetically alike, at least outwardly. And without further information, it was as if Brigid had disappeared without a trace, just like her painting. Kate wanted more; she needed more information. She had a deep-seated desire to understand how that affair had literally begun in the Flannagan's own back yard. And what had happened after that.

And as she stood there pondering, she began to realize how those splotches of colors all over their third-floor attic had come to pass. How clever her parents had been after all in the way they had steered her in another direction. Even though they couldn't hide the fact that her father had grown up in the shadow of Captain James Flannagan.

Suddenly, her father's reaction to her youthful desire to become an artist, made perfect sense. At the time, he must have thought of her career path as the road to perdition.

What folly, she thought; everything she hadn't known or needed to know, was now completely entangled with her present-day baggage.

"Angus is gone, the Gardner paintings are gone, but God willing I can find *Summer Dreams* for you, Gran," Kate whispered like a prayer, "and if heaven does exist, we'll meet one day and you can give me your version of what really happened. I have a feeling it's a doozy."

Chapter 6

In the days and weeks that had turned into three years since Angus's miscalculated adultery (yes, he'd had the crazy notion that she wouldn't notice), Kate had been reliably transported to her childhood and her ability to remember every scene and retain every slight. Back then, that reliability had been second nature. Her teachers had called her 'gifted' and her parents had called her trouble. If they skipped words during story time or if a familiar meal contained a new ingredient, or if her father changed the color code on his buoys, she vocalized her concerns. It was a precociousness that pertained to just about everything throughout her youth. And it seemed as if some of that had followed her into adulthood. Even going so far as being able to use the legal system to hold Angus accountable financially, which had shocked him silly. It had been one of few acts of defiance during their entire marriage.

What remained of this skill or what others hailed as a gift, was the way it also pertained to the Gardner.

Way before the divorce, maybe even when she'd first laid eyes on *El Jaleo*, she had contemplated life through a young Singer Sargent's idealized vision of Spain. Through the years, she had metaphorically chopped the painting into segments. Had she been hoping to emulate his skills or his colors, or was it simply as a way to spur herself on when she felt her talent lagging.

But now, there was Brigid to consider. Kate walked back away from the painting and began to compartmentalize the work to suit this new mindset, beginning with the right side, which seemed to represent her childhood longings. Time spent in a musty attic where she'd played alongside indiscriminate splotches of paint. All those wonderful oranges that had been mixed with explicit blues: shades of paint that went undiminished by time.

And who'd put those paints there in the first place. Colors that aggravated the walls and even the windows that overlooked the island outcroppings and poked at her childish imagination.

Had she been old enough, she might have been more on point about the family secret. The colors that had nothing to do with those in her cardboard box of crayons, but became asterisks on an imaginary page. Or how any of it would have related to scribbles on tattered paper that she'd found that made no sense to a child's brain, but which were clearer today.

In response to her childish questions, her father's face had crumpled, and her mother (aware of Kate's propensities for accuracy) indicated that the room was to be painted and Kate could pick any color she liked.

Giacomo Canelli, had he been available to her, might have been pleased that Kate had retained and for a time, suffered through those left-over pigments. Never making sense of those combinations or how to imitate the brushstrokes he'd so carelessly left behind.

There was a bit of genius in his work, but her father's latest proclamation meant that *Summer Dreams* was still out there somewhere, waiting to be reclaimed. As she stared at *El Jaleo*, there was an ache inside her that suddenly felt bigger than all the nonsense that one misguided husband could cause. She formed a silent promise: to find the missing Flannagan painting no matter what forces lay in her path.

She rested her eyes for a moment and then looked directly at the center of *El Jaleo:* the shadows he'd created to dramatize the scene. Darkness, like the lengthy shadow in *Summer Dreams*, she thought.

She was struck by the idea that the now missing painting might have been hidden away in the bowels of the house while she had spent her childish days rummaging the upstairs.

Those same shadows could also be likened to the soot from their cookstove, and she considered the idea that her parents had had to burn things from the attic that would have made them blush with anxiety.

Moving her eyes all the way left, a figure half in half out of Sargent's scene had always been a good reminder of the way Kate had felt when she had first arrived in the city. She had wanted so badly to be a part of the Boston College collective, that she could still feel the same tentative steps and could almost hear the pounding of an unsure heart.

And more to the point: the sound of dollars flapping in the wind if she failed.

There was no reason in trying to match the threads that pertained to her life with Angus. The years and years they'd managed to fit into this very Spanish story. A themed-event painted by a master craftsman who would never know of her own dreams, but would always be a virtual escape to another time and place.

Sargent's remarkable work flaunted a freedom from inhibitions. Giddiness stabbed at her heart. That old longing quite suddenly egged her to move forward. As if she were the dancer caught in the painter's beam of light. And that light was now blinding. How was it that no one else had ever noticed this, not even during what Maggie had called a cute-meet with Angus. A loveable notion, cozy even, but there was more. And it was important to recognize those facts in order to move forward after today.

In the abstract, Angus was a man who shared a likeness as Irish as her father's unevenly chiseled face. Minus the diminishing hairline that linked all the Flannagan men. But he was also a long-standing employee of the *Boston Globe*, which hadn't immediately fazed her. He was a bread-winner with a regular column and freelance work that paid well, which had pleased her mother a great deal. And made her father stop complaining (at least for a little while). Until he found out that Angus hadn't been able to move Kate away from the foolishness of art. Their relationship had only solidified her desire to create and with even more fervor.

An unexpected element had been added that she would never have told her parents: a vociferous reaction from Moses Lilac (a self-described sartorial king of the Greenwich Village set), and a man so unusual she had memorized everything: he was a chin bobber with a perpetually raised eyebrow; his hands were accent marks to every sentence he spoke. He was not only a colorful character, which could have pertained to his ribald stories, his wardrobe, or his voice that seemed to have been meant for a sports announcer, but he was in fact, Kate's closest confidante at BC. And sometimes even her conscience. And the day she'd described what had happened inside the Cloister, his reaction had nearly broken her eardrums: *Angus Larabee—that tall hunk who writes those sardonic art columns, the same guy who has a thing for Gucci loafers!*

Then, sotto voce: *The man's much too old for you, sweety.*

Yet it was the reference to Angus's shoes and not the way Moses had gushed, that managed to snag her attention. It hadn't taken long for her to equate those Italian shoes with dancing. Without any effort, she had pictured them out and about in Boston proper.

Could see their feet skimming highly polished maple floors that would never meet the rubber-soled boots of Hull Islanders.

Her imagination went so far as sipping drinks with unusual names, but definitely without tiny umbrellas. But instead of some fancy establishment, they'd gone directly to Angus's second-floor condo situated off Newbury Street.

He liked to say he lived on the fringe. She had thought he meant financially, when in fact it was because his condominium was more or less around the corner from the many nineteenth century brownstones that had made Back Bay famous.

Not long after, that location proved far more important to Kate than the idea of wealth accumulating around streetcorners; he seemed to have enough of his own. The condo was an easy walk to shops and restaurants, but more importantly, close enough to a couple of commercial art galleries. Thus, leading to daydreams of having her own work on display. She went so far as to introduce herself to gallery owners who seemed to take a shine to a bit of Hull Island frankness; she was after all, a newbie to the art scene.

And with all that going on, she still found time to torture herself about how many other women he might have lured back to such a masculine warren. Had they been full-fledged artists who were already installed in those same galleries, she'd wondered while trying to maintain her cool? Being cool was very important back then.

His rooms were filled with furniture that suited his size, which forced Kate to focus on the foolishly small kitchen—who besides her would want to cook in a space the size of a boat galley.

There was an original Warhol (bequeathed it seemed) that he'd leaned against the living room wall for no apparent reason except to be a conversation piece, but instead it shamed the monochrome prints on the wall above. She'd had the good sense to keep her own painted sketches out of sight until she felt there might be many more days and nights together.

He was smooth. He was glib, and he could be inarticulate. And on that first night together, he'd been both. They'd drunk an unpretentious red from an adequate stash of bottles stored near his prized turntable (also bequeathed).

They had listened to ballads by a throaty singer, a man she imagined having a cigarette hanging from the corner of his mouth at all times. Angus had hummed along and beamed at Kate while saying all the right things. He was sophisticated and boyish simultaneously and had taken her into a well-timed embrace and let the music move them hypnotically in small circles until desire took over. Like in the films she enjoyed.

And not long after, her ordinary shoes began to cohabitate with those much-talked-about loafers at the bottom of his closet, until it all became about a different dance. And the heights of desire that could be achieved in the middle of an afternoon on a bed made for dancing to the end of love.

The hum of an air conditioner, their bodies floating toward sleep, Angus lazily tracing little dots and dashes on her yoga-flattened belly. He would gift all of her limbs with a sort of rapid-fire shorthand, as if she too were worth writing about: squiggles that formed patterns that in real-life turned into lengthy columns earmarked for the Arts section of the *Globe*.

In that first summer of love, the man with the familiar Irish countenance and perfect teeth and longish hair that quarreled with his collar, had fulfilled her nighttime dreamscape and then some.

The age difference hadn't come into play until years later when she had decided that living together was no longer in fashion. And since she had already obtained the status of a common-law wife. Perhaps he'd looked in the mirror and wondered if he could prolong the situation (he was still turning heads), but with less coaxing than she had imagined, they finally tied the proverbial knot and carried on as usual.

It was too bad that Moses had already dropped out of BC and fled to Paris to find himself in the world of haute couture. This was even more unfortunate because he really would have admired the way she rearranged the bold colored Warhol and placed it in a painted niche on a robust shelf above the turntable.

But she had been too preoccupied with being a wife with self-imposed expectations, to remember to write. So not only was he unaware of the casual visit to City Hall, and the storebought daisy bouquet that Kate had carried, or the circle of life wedding band (instead of a Claddagh like her mum had worn on her wedding day), but he'd missed the opportunity to be her only attendant. And to swoon over their wedding lunch at Casa Romero afterward.

Moses had known from day one how desperately her ring finger had itched for that symbolic ring, but no one had ever been told that even in her teens, Kate had been madly infatuated with the comfortable, loving, yet noisy relationship her parents shared before her mother passed away. Before the wedding cake of a house was left to wheeze with pain.

And the rest of the leavings strewn around the yard—the retired traps and buoys, no longer the paraded-out colors of a seaman—content to haunt the weeds.

Chapter 7

Memories piled upon memories. Kate's little wellies had not only clomped the stairs but stomped the attic floor when she couldn't make sense of those color-stained walls. It would take years before she learned that what looked to be one of her mother's recipes on an old scrap of paper, was in fact a formula written in Giacomo Canelli's hand. This had stayed fixed in her mind as had so many of the other visuals during that stage in her life. By the time she saw the photo of *Summer Dreams*, she had already surmised that there was more to the colors that he'd used for his shadows. Secrets and lies, maybe, or an abounding but unrequited love, who could know? But matching his orange hue had turned into an obsession, a precursor to the most bothersome things that had little to do with real life.

Angus and his burgeoning ego had fallen into that unintended trap. Had made too much of a point of disparaging Sargent's work: *why didn't he make that woman's dress the same color orange?* She had followed his index finger across the painting, knowing how much she loved the painted fruit and the dress for the very reasons that he didn't.

And even though her naivete was still clinging like the morning mist off the ocean at the time, she shot an answer back—in a small voice. Until she realized he was actually longing for someone to do battle with and over the most innocuous subjects.

Fast forward to three years ago on a sultry afternoon, which had turned their kitchen cubical into a walk-in oven. Kate could still picture her hair, as frizzy as a bird's nest, her recipe book open, its pages dampened by perspiration, and the ingredients for a no-bake pie. Angus, wearing a midnight blue t-shirt, jeans, and a pair of those damnable loafers—sans socks as always—had walked in and kissed her on the cheek. He reeked of Bergamot.

To anyone else, he might have been out shopping and been spritzed—as the counter girls were wont to do, especially at the Prudential Mall. And especially to a handsome man who might be looking for a gift.

But to Kate, in the throes of creating something appreciable, that particular scent—a cloying, colorless orange—had quite suddenly begun to smell like the beginning of the end of their marriage.

At which point, she'd found the octave that had been missing out of an earlier respect for his eardrums. Not that day, however. That day, she had dug deep and scooped out every curse that had been tailor-made for the seamen on the Flannagan side.

She had shocked Angus with words he hadn't known she possessed but which somehow came to her quite naturally. Due, she supposed, to all those rousing summer nights when fishing families gathered around a barbecue with tales of yore and all that other stuff she hadn't wanted to be bothered with.

But not even loudly spewed words could change the outcome of that day in the kitchen with Angus. And now, staring at *El Jaleo*, she realized that she had come full circle. She turned away from the painting to give her eyes a rest.

Angus's eyes—as deep as a northern sea—had always compelled her to jump in. She would miss that, and the predictability of a life that had inched forward in normal increments during their relationship, as if preordained.

Theirs was a partnership that had been full of coin tosses and paradoxes and things that were untidy and happen in all relationships. She would miss those too.

If she closed her eyes tight, she could still feel the effect of unanticipated tenderness. Could summon his many work-related accolades. The inner sanctum of her brain held the columns of their bank account, and their wish lists, which in turn allowed them to expand their horizons.

Kate opened her eyes, and heaved a great huge sigh; putting a nice ribbon around it hardly mattered anymore. He was still gone from her bed—the one place where as a couple they'd been safe from everything beyond those walls.

"But our story had mattered!" Kate defended as if by rote, which she supposed would also have to change. But the conundrum: their marital journey had once been decent and true and larger than life, just like this painting.

Their story, though incomplete, lived within every cell and fiber of her being; it would always be there; in her imagination or in real time whenever she returned. It was and always would be a part of the Cloister and her very soul. It lived in the clarity of an Andalusian gypsy dance. Moved within the shadows that swirled and the genius of light. And the spot of color—just so.

Unforgettable moments would be juxtaposed with whatever else was imposed on her whenever she saw this painting. Moments of bearing witness in real time during a honeymoon she had waited years to claim: a week in Spain roaming the countryside, and touring the bars for the sound of flamenco.

Of seeking out the best and worst guitarists who would attempt to play "Malaguena" over the roar of a crowd. Listening keenly through open doorways for heels pounding on wooden floors, and drinking plenty of Spain's renown sherry to soothe the throat from the aftermath of thin cigarettes that had taken their fancy.

And like an Irish blessing, there were no critics between the sheets.

His touch, as his long fingers mapped the terrain of her soft skin and sharp angles; the way her hand fit the nape of his neck as she whispered her need in his ear.

The way his deeply blue eyes smoldered; the fact that she had been made whole by silence from a man who'd made his living with words, was astonishing.

Kate's fingers stiffened; she'd been holding herself together physically. *El Jaleo* had been her north star, and the painting had represented an exciting and slightly exotic future with Angus. Until that peculiar moment in the kitchen when everything had gone up in a puff of yesterdays. And all because of the telltale scent of infidelity.

Had she failed to recognize what had been right in front of her nose, or had Moses been far more prescient than she'd wanted to believe. His great thundering voice was already raising hell with the chorus of bystanders taking a foothold alongside her doubts: how could it be that she was still beckoned to the painted stage—to wear a dash of orange. To provocatively lift a skirt—to celebrate in a bygone tavern!

To breathe in what could only be called timelessness as she made her way across the stone floor in order to reimagine a kiss under the Moorish arch at the end of the room. How in heaven's name was she supposed to forget all of that!

As if Angus had read her thoughts, she felt a pulse-like sensation against her hip. The odd chorus froze in midair and her instincts told her that this was not just a subtle nudge to ensure that she wouldn't forget him. She knew him well enough to know that he was hoping she would be right where he'd pictured her to be standing. It was where he would have been had they not been divorced. It was the eighteenth of March, after all.

The vibration persisted and she grabbed for the phone, ready to make him disappear. She looked around, hoping she was alone because it felt so right to yell out, "Go to hell!" Unfortunately, that left her with the lower lip quiver—it happened so often these days. This was followed by *the* perfect teardrop that poked precariously at her thick lashes. If she moved even a smidgen, the tear would rain down the side of her face and a chain reaction would follow and become what her mother used to call Kate's 'ugly' cry.

"*Oh, my!*"

The voice of an actress on British TV? Certainly not as posh as the Queen. But a definite accent nonetheless. Kate quickly drew the shawl back around her shoulders, and with the tip of her finger, caught the offending tear before it could give her away.

Then, because she suddenly felt a little bit country, she readjusted the soft folds to look the way it had on the display mannequin at TJ Maxx. Maggie had insisted on an outing to Cook's Corner in Brunswick before Kate's re-entry to city life. To which, Kate had added kitchen whatnots, and salty, garlicky snacks. Shopping was tiresome. And so were nights alone.

"Unbelievable," said the man who had boldly sidled into Kate's personal space, his right arm waving with the urgency of a first-time viewer. "Bloody amazing!"

He was windblown. His sallow skin creased, parched looking, but certainly not in the same league as the woman who quickly stepped in to close the gap and eyed Kate with suspicion.

Slithered into a cardinal-red dress with matching lipstick and wearing black pointy-toe heels, she appeared to preen. Perhaps an offering of things to come? Kate couldn't help but wonder if he was brave enough to handle it. But at least this whole scenario had prevented her from having a meltdown.

Or, she thought, they could be actors out on their own for the day, testing their skills on an unsuspecting audience.

"Enjoy," said Kate, but without much heart. They looked at each other and then back at her. *Bad Manners* seemed to be hovering over their heads like a dialogue cloud in cartoon, or some kind of teachable moment for young children.

Then she unwrapped her shawl, in part to quell the heat that had recirculated, and partly to ease the hostility, as if she'd been carrying an invisible weight around her shoulders. Her lips parted as she thought about saying something that wouldn't blow up British diplomacy. They too seemed to be hanging onto words that hadn't been said: the excuse so important that she absolutely had to leave in such a terrible hurry.

Kate felt her face reddening and tried to focus on the English woman's hair, which was luxurious and worthy of a compliment. Something to have them thinking kindly about Americans in general; she had been paying attention to the nightly news after all.

But just as she was about to remark on those dark wavy locks, she realized that they framed the woman's face in the same manner as Brigid's appeared in the photograph and her mind went on an untimely tangent.

Had Brigid preened for Canelli, Kate wondered. Had her grandmother experienced the type of love that inspired poets and songwriters. A woman who in her day, would have put this English woman to shame.

Kate was beyond helping herself now. She swept a hand through her own thick curls and tossed them away from her neck as if a stage waited somewhere—and she needed to be there ahead of the crowd. She was the new diva on the block, able to imagine the barriers of sadness falling away, but without a thought to the tears that had begun to slide down her face after all. The strangers stared at her as if imagining a way to put a stop to such an embarrassment.

But how could she tell them about the woman who was meant to be there for her after her mum died. The grandmother who'd been absent her whole entire life. The one person who could make sense of the secrets hidden within *Summer Dreams*.

As if urging her on, the woman in red coughed lightly. But again, how could Kate reiterate what it felt like to be foolish. Or for that matter, that she'd never intended to be a third wheel—*for anything,* which she hadn't as yet had a chance to say to anyone.

It was only because of Angus that she had entered into a social morass that would require a guidebook to work her way through the norms of 2018.

Moving slightly away from his lady friend, the Englishman smiled at Kate, the reassuring smile of an older brother, and said, "Don't let us chase you off, please."

Kate felt her right foot tug at her as if she might curtsy out of sheer relief. But then, she simply maneuvered her shawl back into place, and said, "You're really not; I've stayed here too long as it is."

And before any more words could be exchanged, she walked the last of her common sense over to the stairs that led to the second-floor galleries. And especially the Dutch Room and the art that would always be an easier fit.

Chapter 8

1936

June 21
Dear Diary,
One day when I look back at these pages, I hope the words will prove worth the effort of putting them under lock and key. I haven't written for a long time, but I desperately need to find some peace among my wayward thoughts. James Flannagan is a mean son-of-a-bitch. I'm not sure I'm strong enough for this life, and I don't know how I'll manage as the days pass, except for those blanketed in fog. It's a coastal thing, and the only benefit that I can see is the disappearance of his ship amidst the clamor of a faraway buoy. The clamminess intrudes everywhere in the house. Into the smallest corners and on the floors and furniture. It blots out my sanity and makes me want to run away, but I kept the cookstove going as I'd learned to do per HIS specifications. Thankfully, he's not here to fault me because that's his favorite pastime. My hands are already raw from scrubbing his filth from the floors; the man is unkempt and foul, and I can't get the stink out of the bedsheets no matter how hard I scrub.

Just think, if he cared about the attic too, I might be dead by thirty. Having two floors to clean is more than enough, but I am still intrigued by what might be up there.

And thank God for my new friend, Helen. She has a habit of dropping by and she did that again today, which is why I guess I've decided to start these ramblings again. To document what has been taking place in case something happens to me. Dramatic, you might say, but I'm a practical woman too. Evil lurks in this house and no amount of cleaning can wipe it away. It doesn't really have a name, or does it?

When I ran into Helen at the general store, I mentioned that James would be away, and I'm so glad that I did. She turned up unexpectedly and with the same gift I'd had in mind for Tommy, but hadn't gotten around to buying. James keeps an eye on my household monies too.

It was only a little tinker toy, but it's something he couldn't easily break. And at first his face lit up with a smile that would light the world. And then I noticed a frown forming as he took the toy into his room. And that's when it dawned on me that Tommy was being hard on his things to compensate for the way his father was with him. That hateful man should never have been allowed to spread his seed in the first place!

Helen had noticed the change in my expression and looking at me she put a finger to her lips and took off after Tommy. When she came out of his room, she was all smiles. She said that Tommy reminded her of her baby brother who was now a man of twenty-five.

Years from now, when Tommy is all grown, I'll look back on this page and remember this pretty woman and the way she tried to help my son grow into a fine young man too. Because what more could I ask of him.

So, besides all her wisdom, she also brought eggs from her own hens, and I immediately made us a scramble since I hadn't eaten a thing that morning. And that too was my husband's fault.

But best of all, she brought some much-appreciated town gossip, which included a few little tidbits about James. Not that I care what others think, since I have enough issues to deal with, but sometimes it helps to know I'm not too far off the mark in my opinions. Besides, what others think of him can't be worse than what I know to be true.

I already feel that Helen and I are growing close, and I know that if I didn't have her to talk to, I'd go a little batty. And I'd never know anything about the goings on around this shiny coastline—not so different and yet it might as well be hundreds of miles from the Boothbay peninsula and Tim, my first and only boyfriend.

And yet each time I let myself dwell on Tim (and I haven't told her any of that yet), I rage over the high and mighty Bo Gallaher who used to make Tim stand in the dooryard like the man who brought the wood. Like all the workmen and delivery people as if they meant nothing except what they could do for him. Is it any wonder that I overlooked this pattern of behavior when I was first introduced to James. Although he concealed it well enough at first. And of course, with captaining a ship, it seemed natural that he would bellow his requests rather than ask politely for anything.

But that long-standing feud between the Gallaghers and the Nelsons over a spit of posted land, topped whatever love my father may have had for me. And as God is my witness, I have paid with my flesh and bones. Far too high a price to be shackled to a man like James, and I am only now seeing that. So, what is wrong with me, you might ask. Heartbreak over what I'd left behind—too many romantic notions from the movies I've seen—too many novels? All I know is that I landed here, on this island that bears up well under drama. It has the bleached rocks and ragged edges to attest to that, while Helen sees something else. To her, the island offers up another form of romance as in the quieter tide pools as yet unseen by others. Or within ancient summer cottages in places like Christmas Cove, which by the way, seems to turn up everywhere along the various coastal indentations.

But there's no tenderness in the lapping waves or the screech of gulls or the mudded roads for me. There is only a handful of hate to spread on top of the dirt that James leaves behind.

I'm chattel and nothing more and in 1936 of all things!

And Mother's no better, almost subservient. I think she really hoped I would be the same so that she wouldn't look so bad. But that's not how it works, I know that now.

I also believe that I would have been different had Tim and I been allowed to court, not that I knew back then what type of man would make a well-rounded husband, but he certainly would have been kinder than my father and far better than a man like James, that's for sure.

Mark my words, dear diary, I will never forgive my parents for what they've done.

And Helen, bless her heart, she may not have a husband and is caring for a daft mother and an ancient cat and a house almost as draughty as mine, but she has known love on a far different scale from anything I've even imagined.

And right now, she is the only person I can confide in and hopefully trust, because I've already said more to her than I've ever said to anyone about my marriage. Life is perfectly abysmal like this and Helen is so much stronger, and besides, she's really good with Tommy. That has to count for something, right?

But what do I do next? How can this be all there is: James, this behemoth of a house, the smell of the sea. It's funny to watch people along the shoreline raising their noses to the briny perfume. Songs are sung, and I'm told that poets claim it for their own purpose more often than not.

But those tellers of tales and shanties, the men who raise a glass and a song, don't have to live with a man like James Flannagan.

Even Helen claims the salt air is filled with a refreshing tang, good for the skin and nasal passages.

While month after month, the brininess that walks in on the heels of the man I have come to loathe, lingers within this house like the smell of rot.

Chapter 9

2018

Kate had left the Cloister, but it was Katherine who held her head high as she walked into the Dutch Room. This wasn't a room for foolish tears, she thought, as her eyes perused the walls. The artwork in here was less boisterous, though not less colorful than what she'd left behind. But the pieces mounted on the walls were more regal in content: a portrait of a queen, an earl, and a doctor of law, to name a few. But unlike *El Jaleo*, those portrayed here appeared static, immovable and without any flare whatsoever. Had this been intentional, she wondered. After all, they had kingdoms to rule and books to write and wars to fight. Of course, she thought of the Brits; how could she not. But would they appreciate the painting of the lowly painter's apprentice that had been placed among all this royal personage. For Kate, Rembrandt van Rijn's portrait stood a cut above all the other paintings. He had painted the robe he couldn't earn with a title, though he'd earned a place among them here at the Gardner. His gentle face continued to offer the compassion Kate had become used to and needed, especially today. And as always, she sought his eyes, took in his expression—guileless, as if he'd been expecting her.

Anything beyond her own feelings and impressions about the artist's history was available to anyone through Google: the names of his family, and that he happened to be Isabella's first major acquisition. Kate had done due diligence regarding all available facts and had retained photos from many old newspapers that pertained to the heist and commentary during various March anniversaries.

Over time, Rembrandt had become her personal hero, and more importantly, his self-portrait continued to remain on the North Wall, gilded, and beguiling as ever. What was always a shock to her was the fact that he was still there. He was prominent among the emptiness, the frames that would most likely never be filled with their original occupants. The walls hushed by what had taken place.

She'd been about to walk across the room when she heard a tapping of shoes. She turned to see that a lone woman stood in the doorway, her face turning this way and that as if searching for someone. She spotted Kate staring and turned her head away as if she too couldn't be bothered with small talk today.

Kate watched, grateful in her own way. But she needn't have worried. This woman went directly to the portrait of Mary I, Queen of England, the Tudor Queen. A woman with a smile that was both beguiling and sinister.

Kate looked from the portrait to the new visitor. There was the tiniest resemblance in their oval faces and reddish hair and when she caught Kate staring again, she flashed a tight-lipped smile that could not disguise a similar dimple in her chin.

And then, as if taunting Kate, the stranger centered herself in front of the queen's portrait, and did what Kate hadn't had the guts to do: perform a minor curtsy. *Oh, my god,* Kate thought as if the whole royalty thing could be contagious. Should she run back downstairs after all, she wondered, tell those Brits what had just happened. Or just tuck it away for a lovely story to tell at a dinner party—if she ever had one again.

But then she heard footfalls from the floor above, which meant that the room would soon be filled with other admirers and those with a deep curiosity about the existing frames and the story they would each conclude. And Kate still had to pay a proper homage to Rembrandt.

If she lived in the city, she would simply come back another day, but that was no longer an easy option. It had become far more important these days to make the most of the time she had, which also meant she would have to forego a stop at Café G. And a sampling of their newer menu.

It had been her hope to have Maggie along today, and Kate mulled over the idea of inviting the visiting Brits to join her, but quickly changed her mind.

And besides, Rembrandt was watching. His eyes spanned the distance and like any good portrait, they had always managed to find her wherever she stood. They even found her in her dreams.

His face was as gentle as the Earl of Arundel's was haughty. Rembrandt was cloaked in humility; the Earl in battle gear, ready for a fight, as if Rubens had pissed him off. Maybe he had, Kate thought turning to the painting just to her right. But whatever had taken place in the centuries before hardly mattered. There was a keenly developed, yet inexplicable, kinship with Rembrandt to be reimagined.

Barely able to curate her own life, Kate stood in awe each and every time at the way in which this room had been curated. She no longer painted, but she'd always been and still was heavily into color theory. And someone had thoughtfully selected a perfect backdrop for van Rijn, and they had done this with an eye toward complimenting every other painting within the Dutch Room.

The green shade cascaded down the moire-like fabric, the light turning the cloth into a multitude of greens: celery or young pea sprouts or even ripened pears. She was fond of pears and suddenly recalled that she'd painted a bowl of artificial ones for a still life class while in college. That was the year she had turned an oversized pear that she'd found at the grocery store into a drawing that looked like a woman's butt, which one of her classmates had called a pint-sized Botticelli.

Kate had gifted the finished painting, done on a miniature-sized canvas, to a friend to hang in her kitchen. It was fate, of course, because by that time, she was well aware that the small painting would be the only one to ever 'go public'.

And even though today might be considered one of those fake spring days in the northeast, this room and that odd mix of green, screamed the coming of her favorite season.

Plus, the room was filled with Italian furniture that she wished she could build a house around.

Kate had spent years going through the various galleries. She had tried to absorb as much as possible from the variety of work, both art and sculpture, and what had begun with her silly pear painting, had turned into a true affinity for the Botticelli's.

After that, her attention turned to Titian's *Europa,* and then the painted virgins. That love was followed by her romance with the divine cherubs holding small bows and arrows who had seemed destined to watch over the museum guests from above.

And as time went on, the art became conclusive proof that her own figurative work would never make the grade. No matter how many hours spent or how many live models she was cajoled into drawing.

In the end, it all came down to color. Her true calling. And beyond the many shades of orange that addled her brain from time to time, she had locked onto the blue paint Isabella had chosen for the hallways. And like a chain reaction, she developed a penchant for works by Vermeer. And she had chosen a print of the *Girl with the Pearl Earring* because that blue mimicked the blue here at the Gardner. A blue developed by an Italian architect prominent in another era.

And suddenly Kate remembered the blue swatches of paint in her childhood playroom and wondered if Canelli had been a devotee of that particular Italian. She had tried, but still hadn't actually pinpointed the mixture Canelli had used for the painting in the photograph that was the only proof of its existence. And now, she couldn't even try to match it, because she had left the photo at home.

Her brain began to feel as if it would short-circuit: the lengthy train ride; Rembrandt and the anniversary; images that couldn't be unseen after the robbery—some more painful than others. Not to mention the ones entombed in the Cloister below.

She was a Flannagan. Irish as well as English blood ran through her veins. But what about Spanish. How else could she explain the way being in that country had touched her so deeply. Who knew what nomad had stowed away in a hold in another century only to find himself on foreign soil, wedded to a new country and an unexpected life.

But this wasn't a contest between *El Jaleo's* panache versus Rembrandt's existence in this place where he had long held court. Both masterpieces had helped put the Gardner on the map. It was so much more. A story to be written, she thought, if she were a writer. Something to be made from her deep-seated desires; the way the art made her feel as if she were the only person to ever lay eyes on it. Or even a story about a woman living alone in a rental that hadn't become a home until she chose to make it so.

She had studied up on Rembrandt; fame hadn't protected him or his collector from the loss of a child any more than conscience had given the people Kate loved, the hope of one. And while he'd never made a point of it, she knew that down deep

Angus had envied the men at the *Globe* who trotted out their kids' photos at every opportunity.

But unlike Rembrandt, she hadn't spent countless hours alone in a darkened room as a silent witness when a stunning Vermeer was ripped from its frame.

Or when Rembrandt's only seascape had been stolen in those wee hours along with others from the Short Gallery and the Blue Room. There were too many scars left behind from that fateful night to be eased into a short story, especially by her.

During the aftermath of the 1990 burglary, a myriad of theories about smugglers and forgers and black markets had unfolded to different audiences in different countries. And yet no one had been caught.

But it got worse. The press—the slash and burn of reputations—more theoretical jabs. Heads would roll. A colossal amount of money was at stake. All that collective handwringing and wild theories that overrode solid news.

To this day, she recalled the way the original story had been served up—never fully digestible. More like a badly written 'whodunnit'.

Cringe-worthy articles, blame cast in all directions, and for Kate, pure and simple relief that Isabella had not lived to rue the day.

Chapter 10

"Mrs. Jack" as Isabella was familiarly known, had an eye for design and a passion for collecting. As a result, the museum was filled with treasures from around the world that she and Jack Gardner sought together prior to his death.

From her very first visit, Kate had felt grounded here at the Gardner and had returned time and again, fascinated by their collection. Envious of all their worldly travels.

But after the robbery, things had changed. And much later, the news became fodder for the curious. Wars had been fought, political parties had exchanged residences; hell, even the gardens at sixteen hundred Pennsylvania Avenue had suffered the indignities of public opinion.

Much had happened on the world stage since the Gardner was established. And here it was twenty-eight years after a heist valued in the millions, and even with "a number of active leads", not one of those stolen pieces had ever been recovered.

Yet Kate believed that *if* the *Globe* had allowed Angus's point of view, there would have been a pithy column to add salt to wounds that always remained fresh.

He'd been hard at work on it when the news was once again front and center in Boston after an old lead had resurfaced, as they often had: connections that leaped from Irish mobs to petty thieves and the possibility of an inside job. Angus had even tried to trace a Michel Rembrandt, who'd been interviewed but thought to be pretending to be a long lost relative.

Back then, she had been certain that Angus's article would have only stirred up more muck, though he'd been unwilling to give in to her pleas to pull back.

What had he hollered? Of course: *then tell everyone to put on their high waders; this needs to be said.* The results were predictable. Just like the knots that instantly coiled somewhere near Kate's sternum, and naturally, this was the day she'd forgotten the antacids.

Instead, she had stuffed the ridiculous excuse for a purse with a couple of tissues and her cell phone, and by extension, the ghostwriter who loved to control the dialog.

It was turning into a very long morning indeed. And as much as she disliked thinking of her very brief stint with therapy, Kate felt the pull of a better angel. The dutiful one with a lopsided halo. The tired-of-it-all woman Angus had traded in for a slim blonde with only a sketchy interest in art. And even though her anger had turned into a tinderbox that could plume into flames at any moment, she knew for a fact that Angus had not been immune to what had happened at the Gardner either. For all his bluster, he adored fine art; he just didn't want anyone to get the upper hand on his work.

But for Kate, the sight of those still empty frames hanging against that same winsome fabric, would always create a visceral reaction. It would stay with her for days afterward, and she doubted that today's ride home would be any different.

She thought of the train ride into Boston, the time spent pondering a Christie novel. Maybe for the train ride home, she'd conjure a 'thriller' that would be based upon the missing Canelli.

She might take a different route and create a map that would locate the criminal who stabbed and robbed a painter back in the thirties and got away with it. Even if not true, it would set Hull Islanders abuzz. A dirty little secret that no one would ever admit to even if it had been true. But they sure would read it!

Imagination was nothing new to Kate; it had always been a coping mechanism; she had a tendency to overthink and readjust as she had done when she moved back to Maine. Today was just an extension of those changes. A new narrative to old situations, ones that had her dialing up some unattractive words, the way that Angus used to when he was hard at work on his creative pursuits.

And the more she thought, the more she realized that she was once again stalling. Savoring the feeling of a face-to-face with Rembrandt. The way she'd done in the Cloister, none of which had to do with the manuscripts Angus had stashed. Files that had been comprised of boxes stacked against the wall of their closet (behind those crazy loafers), before they'd split up, which she might never be able to unsee again.

Kate felt the weight of her stupidity—she had been duped into thinking that he'd simply been too busy with his work to help her do anything back then.

But all that 'busyness' was far more egregious…younger women required a lot of energy, after all.

"Damn it, Angus, picture this why don't you!" Kate's outburst fell onto the floor with a sad little echo. Given its due, the small sound might swell into the beginning outline for a fantastical story, she thought. Something that couldn't be pounded into submission by a wounded ego.

A tale that may or may not have been due to the earlier train ride that portended an imaginary disaster. One that might feature the ever-delightful Poirot or someone like him. Wouldn't that be lovely, she thought, to be able to create fiction that had nothing to do with reality or was remotely connected to her ex.

Angus had never been a fan, but as far as Kate was concerned, the world could use more men like the famous Belgian detective. Or at the very least, someone of his ilk in real life whom she could hire to find *Summer Dreams*. Of course, a man like Poirot would be *the* man to tackle the mystery of the museum's missing artwork.

How easy it was now to picture dear bespeckled Agatha with her fingers poised at her trusty typewriter. Maybe mining her thoughts for "Death on the Nile". Or better still, planning her own escape when she found out that her husband had cheated. "It happens to the best of us." Kate offered to the Earl, who because of her stance, was now to her left, and whose face indicated he would never have a clue.

How had he escaped the robber's blade, she wondered, and then felt terrible for thinking such a thing. Then Kate pictured the mystery writer standing beside her thinking the exact thing, but yet knowing that not even Agatha could have dreamed a better setting for the man with the precise mustache and polished manners. A sometimes-tedious genius who with only a handwritten note at his disposal, would rush to the aid of Mrs. Gardner.

'*Belle*', Kate suddenly recalled. A fondly spoken name for the exacting woman who was considered the damsel of Boston society.

Absolutely no one would be expected to leap off a page in Belle's defense or with greater aplomb than the fictional sleuth, Kate thought. She again conjured up the smart-suited Poirot with his amusing gait making his way into one of the fancy-dress affairs that had been held here in 1903.

It had been three years in the making, but Kate felt herself freed of all constraints. She gazed longingly at the unique flooring—meant for dancing—and she thought of a piece of music that would lend itself to the moment.

And then, her hip vibrated. *NOT AGAIN!*

"Are you one of the filmmakers?" Kate turned, wide-eyed; someone had been watching without her knowledge. "Sorry, I didn't mean to startle you."

Kate noticed a guide's badge hanging on a ribbon around the woman's neck. "It's just that we're expecting the filmmakers…the ones planning a documentary for the anniversary," she said.

"No, it's not that," said Kate. "I *was* making a movie, or at least a story…in my head, and was just about to make a fool of myself, so thank you for bringing me back to earth." Kate thought she caught a wry smile, but the guide replied, "It was my pleasure." And then she began to step away.

"I almost forgot," said Kate stopping the woman in her tracks. "I still can't figure out why they left this Rembrandt behind."

"It's painted on wood," the guide replied without a second thought.

Kate had been staring at the painting forever and a day and suddenly felt very foolish. "Naturally." She looked over at a pedestal, "But what about the rest, the weighty unbendable stuff, like that sculpture over there; same thing right?"

"They disguised themselves as Boston cops," the guide said all the while her eyes were searching the room. "But that doesn't mean they were very bright, and I have no idea if they had people waiting directly outside, or if they'd come with containers or anything that would have been able to be moved in a hurry. All I know is that I don't know how they got away with it."

Kate had long been out of answers, so all she could add was, "Do you think they would have destroyed them to avoid getting caught; after all, it's been so many years?"

"I pray not," were the words that Kate heard just as the guide was about to walk away. But then she turned back to Kate and said, "Don't trip; you've just stepped on your shawl."

Kate hadn't realized that while she'd been concocting an imaginary waltz, she'd let the shawl slip from her pretend evening dress, only to expose mundane leggings instead of more preferable silk stockings.

It seemed as if she'd been adjusting and righting this silly shawl the entire morning and would most likely continue. It may be the last time that she wore the damn thing, she thought as she said, "Thanks, it sure does cover a multitude of sins."

"That's why I wear these outdated peasant blouses," the guide said as she lifted the edge of an ecru-colored hem. "And there's my little group, right on time."

Kate's eyes followed as the woman's glittering rings managed to counter the gray light that had remained fastened on a nearby window. A small entourage had gathered across the hall and a lanky, semi-bald man waved back. "That's my cue; enjoy!"

Kate watched the way the guide strode to the men and women who appeared very anxious to get moving. An air of confidence in her gait, a small sway to her hips, a sense of confidence in the way she held her head. A guide to control the dialogue and set a scene, far better than Kate would do, especially today. "It's time for me to stop, Belle," Kate whispered into the air. "This room rightfully belongs to you."

Chapter 11

Kate had been on a self-imposed hiatus; it seemed best at the time. But without intention, she'd cut herself off, a shut-in without a genuine infirmity. Women her age would scoff at her lack of backbone, her need to fall on her own sword, as if she should have had a better grasp of her marriage. If it weren't for Maggie's intervention, Kate might have been more like Isabella and avoided her community altogether. She might even have worn dark veils to protect herself from prying eyes.

Kate had read somewhere that Isabella had at one time been chauffeured around in a nineteenth century sleigh, dressed in mourning, and bundled against the cold. While her own escape from the public had been behind the tinted windows of Maggie's SUV. Days when Kate was practically dragged out of the house for a ride around Hull Island for some fresh air. Or even as far as Brunswick to check out the stores that she refused to enter.

But unlike Isabella, Kate had no purpose to her own mourning. No grand plans to keep her from thinking about Angus during the first year away from Boston, even for a minute. Frissons of pleasure had disappeared from her life. There had seemed nothing to salvage, not even her own art since she had given that up too.

But what was even worse, was that he'd taken over her dreams, turned them into nightmares. And then he seemed to have absconded from the dark and into the daily chores.

He turned up wherever anger lurked: when she had to patch the back door screen that had taken the brunt of the broom handle. Or mend the broken cups or smashed plates left on the floor during a pathetic rage.

And who else could fix the lid on the inherited 'hope chest' long after those types of hopes had succumbed to reality.

It was Maggie who'd come in to help, to literally pick up the pieces and offer sobering advice along with homemade soup and fudgy brownies.

Until one day, Kate had woken up with an epiphany. It was not necessarily an ambitious one, mind you, but an honest-to-goodness need to clean the house with what after so much time had passed, could only be called abandon. There was deftness to her moves: rooting dust bunnies from their lairs; grabbing cobwebs in all shapes and sizes. Creeping through the many creepy things that had formed while she had slept away her inability to cope.

And during all that time, she had muffled Angus's dramatic outbursts with new ones of her own. Until one day, the corners he'd tried to claim were empty of his shadowy presence. The sound of his imaginary footsteps had been trampled by her own stronger ones. Small pleasure could be found in her wanderings around the richness of a landscape filled with wonder. Energy renewed in small doses like the medicine her mother would dole out when Kate was a child.

She even discovered a small bundle of well-scrubbed paintbrushes that had been stuffed inside an old tee shirt and placed under the kitchen sink. There'd been no rhyme or reason to her unpacking when she had first moved in, but in her altered state of mind, it's amazing that she hadn't put the brushes in the oven!

She hadn't unwrapped them…yet. But now as she gazed at Rembrandt, she wondered if he might very well applaud the idea, this unexpected flutter of excitement that could be felt welling up inside her chest.

What would Rembrandt think of the idea of challenging herself again? Maybe to think outside the box. And instead of painting figures and plain fruit, to dig out some of the whatnots with flare that had belonged to her mother. Many of which had to be stored away when her father had moved to the assisted living facility in Brunswick.

Or maybe, like everyone else since she'd begun her artistic journey, Rembrandt might have told her to forego those very youthful and quite lofty ambitions, and get a 'real' job.

Chapter 12

Were Kate to actually concoct a story, this is where she might begin: the screenwriters have left behind one man with a camera. Music (the type that Kate would dance to) causes him to slide toward stage left where three fresh-faced college girls wearing sweatshirts that are similar to those from her own college days. He swings the camera and catches their giggles, the way they bend to each other as they examine one of the more explicit plaster figures. Behind them there is a new patter of voices as more people glide through the doorways.

And the furniture: the setting for whatever a smart documentarian needed in order to bring the film to life. The perfect backdrop for anyone who knew anything at all about staging. Kate pictured a moving panoply of museum goers, their voices mingling seductively with a soft background sound. A waltz or even a light-footed fox trot.

Today had started as a dramatic event and was still building into more drama. Her own misguided attempt to create something out of nothing, and now she couldn't help herself. She glided toward the walnut cabinet, being sure not to lean in too close in case the perfume left a shadow of evidence.

In doing so, her spirit lightened up but she was also more aware that she was still drawing out the face-to-face with Rembrandt. She couldn't say exactly why, except that to savor each and every moment with the man she considered her personal hero seemed appropriate now that she was no longer able to just pop in on him and all the other pieces of fine art as she once had.

Later, during the train ride home, she'd have time to dissect and disseminate and maybe make more sense out of her actions. The spinning of memories; blending one thought until it became paragraphs that would become food to live on while she was in Maine. Learning the process of adapting to her new life in any way that she could.

And then she made a small misstep: she saw her reflection in the window panel. Her jaw dropped. Just when had she decided it was appropriate or even necessary to wear shawls or bulky sweaters or anything that would disavow her womanly figure. And when had she taken such a liking to the freshly baked bread that seemed to be directly related.

And on top of that, a world of skinny jeans awaited—not that she needed to be as thin as the BC girls, but how would she ever find out if she continued to carry on this way. But before she could go down that rabbit hole, she thought as she headed to the Ladies Room, she needed to find a proper mirror.

By the time Kate re-entered the Dutch Room, her hair looked less of an afterthought. Her lips were glossed a shade of pink from a tube that had been stuck in the seam of the far too dainty purse. But the hunger remained, as if Café G had just served up a batch of fresh buns to their waiting customers, which of course given the hour of the day, they probably had. She swallowed the thought and headed directly for the Old Master. It was important now to get ahead of the crowd that could be heard swelling just outside the gallery. Most likely another tour and Rembrandt would be their first stop.

She thought of the earlier experience with *El Jaleo*, the way the painting assumed the shouts of *ole* from an adoring crowd and her heels hit the floor tile with a bit more abandon. A staccato-like sound reminiscent of better days and better times. Rembrandt, on the other hand, had always seemed to whisper 'handle with care', especially to this audience of one. Today would not be any different. Except today she had more questions for him: had he, like many starving artists of that period, suffered his craft. She certainly had—agonizing over every line and form. Would he have been as good a teacher as he was an apprentice to another master painter. Or would he have praised her flaws like one of her teachers in order to gloss over their own.

If she cared at all to be brutally honest, Angus may have saved her from all of that by loving her no matter her lack of talent.

Rembrandt, or at least his painting, had been saved as well—twice in fact. First by Isabella's protégé, a Mr. Berenson who'd found the portrait in the nick of time before it went into the National Gallery.

And again, during the robbery in 1990. "Or we would never have met," Kate whispered as soon as she was standing directly in front of him.

As always, she diligently scanned every angle of his portrait. She assumed the stance of an artist and diagnosed the paint colors that had become so important to her: a mix of light gray and brown that had appeared almost green from a distance. And how they related to the moire fabric behind him.

When she'd been new to Boston, and been particularly homesick, Rembrandt's colors had reminded her of the greenish underbelly of a wave scooping up the sand as it came to shore.

The intrigue of color had never left her, not even when she'd left the city. Instead, she had become bolder in her choices, and in the way she'd decorated. The only place she was lacking was in her wardrobe.

But Rembrandt had gone beyond mere color; he'd used the wooden tip of his brush to create the finite touches that hadn't been quite as obvious as they were today.

She had failed at the impasto technique as well. And each time she studied his portrait she found something new, like the way the highlights from an unknown source managed to pick out the details of his facial hair.

There was a softness to his shadow work as well. Today, his eyes looked more unsure than ever, she thought, but maybe she was projecting.

Today, especially, the hat made him appear as if he'd failed to take into consideration the nobility that a feathered bonnet would exude.

She thought of the disappearance of *The Storm on the Sea of Galilee*. Taken on this very day decades ago. Who would be singing its praises now; who would appreciate his only seascape and the way his depiction of water and waves had made her feel as if she too had been hanging on for dear life.

Unlike her mother, Kate loved the feel of saltwater on her skin. The tang on her tongue when a wave slapped her face as she lifted a trap from the cold ocean. But then again, she'd never been out in the raging storms the way her ancestors had. Never had to fight to hold on for dear life until there was nothing left to hold on to—like Brigid's husband, James.

Everything she had ever loved about the exploration of art—with Angus as well as with her friend Moses, had changed. And with them out of the picture, she had started communing with Rembrandt. And he had unwittingly become her comfort. A silent confidante in an increasingly noisy world. And now, things were changing once again.

Would he have been proud that her interest in art hadn't died completely, she thought even though it was a nonsensical idea. Unless she believed in the afterlife. But in truth, she half expected to see an argument on his lips...to chastise her for everything she *hadn't* done. Or for allowing something as commonplace as a failed marriage to keep her from returning to the Gardner before now.

Overridden with misplaced guilt, overthinking things that could bring her to a halt before she'd even touched the surface: commentary from a therapist who was concerned that Kate worried too much—because her brain revisited everything.

Of course, it made sense. Kate had projected her own thoughts onto someone who obviously couldn't refute anything said or thought. Unlike the man she had married.

Rembrandt was and would always be protected by his silence. It was what made him so important, this staring at her from the safety of his place on the wall. What would he have thought of *Summer Dreams,* she pondered. And especially the artist who'd painted it.

Would the two men have been *sympatico* in their artistic thinking. Or just competitors. And what of *Summer Dreams,* she wondered yet again. Why had that painting been kept out of sight all through her childhood. Would it have made a difference to her own artistic license if she'd had that as a reference during those first years.

Her mother kept a collection of gold-trimmed red glass on the mantlepiece. Seasonally, she changed them out for the yellows, pinks and blues in a mix-match of shapes and sizes that would catch the morning sun. The wall above would have been perfect to host the Flannagan painting. But it never had appeared there, not once.

Kate released a slow breath. The Hull Island house had borne lasting traces of the sea: shells adorned the window sills; a ship's bell hung in the dining room; a pair of worn oilskins hung from a hook in the garage; photographs of grandfather Flannigan's schooner remained by the kitchen door until one day Kate bumped it and the glass smashed to pieces. Her father never put it back.

In spring, the windows were flung open. Tasks were assigned. Lemon scented the furniture and pine, the floors. Apples and berries were picked. Pie plates were taken down from the cupboard. Tablecloths were brought out of storage, ironed and folded to wait for Sunday celebrations.

The entire house was filled to the brim with her mother's creative touches and valued bric-a-brac. And yes, even her father's noise—on the stairs, in the yard, and bellows over the back embankment that always misrepresented his size.

It wouldn't take a trained therapist to realize that Kate had wanted to reclaim the family homestead in order to force an unrealistic situation onto Angus. To fill the house with their own belongings because without recognizing the signs at the time, their marriage was already on life support.

Kate studied Rembrandt's face anew. Was there such a thing as a distinct line between brain and brush, because he had somehow painted his own vulnerability. What did her face look like, she wondered now that her heart was being wrenched dry of its memories. Would her eyes and brow indicate all that useless freight she'd been carrying around. Or would her hips bear the brunt of the cravings that she couldn't feed fast enough.

Or could this be enough, this simply being here in the moment. To acknowledge that Rembrandt, in lieu of the other important men in her life, had become for whatever illogical reasoning, *her* guy. For it's what she always felt in his presence.

She might conjure many thoughts about what his life would be like in today's day and age, but that wasn't the point of being here. It had to do with his watchful silence. He listened—and for now that had to be enough.

Chapter 13

1936

Brigid studied the lock that kept her secrets away from prying eyes; she inserted the key. Then, she sat on her bed and composed a new entry.

Dribbles in a stream drying up, rustles of leaves underfoot, July without rain. There'd been so much fog and damp for so many weeks, and now we've been reduced to conserving our well water. So instead of mopping up after I settled Tommy with his toys, I took to the attic to see what needed to be done. I finally gave in to it, trudged up those stairs while balancing my cleaning supplies. I banged my knee against a tread, water spilled from my pail and I repeated some of the words that James likes to fling at me. But I had to go up there. I kept worrying that James would get it into his head that I absolutely had to clean it, even though he'd never bothered before. But he is as changeable as he is insufferable. Like the way he dreams up other chores for me to do. Why didn't you make a pie he'd say or why haven't you polished my Sunday shoes. All the while he's cursing the gods for one thing and another, never ever seeming pleased about returning home to be with us.

The steps to the attic are meant for childlike feet, steep, but obviously wide enough to handle the leather chair that I found pushed under an eave. The attic was dirty but in an abandoned way and easy to wipe down. Not in a moldy way like so much of the house below. And then it occurred to me that the attic may have been an add-on to the house, like me.

James has never seemed to care how I spend my days, just that I'm where I'm supposed to be in the night, which revolts me to no end. A woman's duty, he says, though I doubt he understands the part he's supposed to play. His breath is foul, his words are no better...I don't know how long I can bear it.

And now that I've seen the attic's potential, maybe I can find escape on the days he's away. Someplace that has no claim on James, no tangible evidence he's been up there, which could make it mine alone. It offers a wonderful view of the harbor and a pretend life, a world without him in it.

From the moment I saw the slant of the ceilings and the reach of the sky, I was able to imagine what it would be like to lay on the slim cot, stare at the moon on the nights he's at sea. And dream to my heart's content.

I found an old Indian blanket and brought it downstairs. Then, I fixed Tommy his lunch and when he was finished, we took the blanket out to the backyard where he helped me beat the dust out of it with his small fists, and I imagined he was taking out his own hurt, the things he's too young to articulate, on that bit of wool. It's hard to say with a toddler, but it wasn't long before all he wanted to do was play with his toy truck. I had to wait until he tired himself out before I could go back up the stairs with the blanket and a cup of tea. Going up and down these stairs might help me lose some of the weight I'd put on during the winter, maybe even more so than running after a toddler. I dusted off the chair and sat to test the springs and then covered it with the blanket. It looked so tempting that I laid down on the cot and closed my eyes for a few minutes. There's a slight view of Bang Island, if I lean out of the window at a certain angle. But if I try and focus on that spit of a rock, I'll be reminded of rowing out there with Tim and how I thought he'd be the boy I'd marry one day.

And now all I have left are dreams about what might have been. Well, maybe not—thinking of Tim is far too painful.

Maybe it can be my place to dream what might still be!

Dear Diary,

I began dreaming too much, and now it's August and the first chance I've had to be alone with my thoughts. I asked Helen to come up to the attic this morning. I haven't told you much about her, except that she's pretty, but she's also a funny duck, and yet mysterious too. Overly friendly and yet snobbish as well. She croons to Tommy with the voice of an angel, and then spews the words of a guttersnipe raised on the docks. But she has succumbed to the view from my little hideaway and I could see the wheels turning over in her brain, as if she could see herself up there instead of me.

After an hour, I showed her the widow's walk on the other side of the house, the place I have to stand in order to keep an eye out for James. God forbid, he's out there on the Lady Dora spying up at me, but I didn't say that to Helen.

We were dripping wet by the time we came back downstairs which means I'm going to have to pry open a couple of windows without damaging anything or bring the electric fan up from the bedroom. Or both.

Helen and I have made a habit of sitting out back on chairs dragged from the kitchen. She sometimes smuggles in a bottle of wine and we now talk about all the things that I've kept from her, especially my fear of prying eyes. And who knows if James has paid someone to keep an eye on me while he's away.

Helen sometimes gets a little tipsy and then she talks about stuff that she'd do up here if she were in my shoes. She'll wink and I'll pretend that I don't know what she means because I am so mortified.

And now I can't think of anything else.

Chapter 14

2018

Kate jumped back from Rembrandt's portrait. She'd been leaning in so close that her eyes had blurred—next she'd need glasses!

Her sudden laugh came out as a snort. She grinned at the artist and then peeked over her shoulder just in case. Angus might as well have been standing there, prodding her to think outside the hurt, buy the damn glasses, move on, like he'd apparently done.

But had he really? If he were here right this very minute, he would ignore all the stuff and fluff of romance and concentrate on Rembrandt's heavy robe. He'd offer a diatribe that would sound important to the followers of his columns, and then he'd look at her innocently like he had that last time, his words seared on her brain: *you're the artist, is that puce green— it intimates the supposition that being dressed for the manor borne might give him greater appeal to the seventeenth century society he longed to conquer.*

"Damn." Rembrandt didn't flinch, but he should have, she thought; this was another one of Angus's pompous statements that continued to pour through her as if by osmosis.

But this was also where the best memories corroded; she'd lied to Angus by omission back when she'd had the perfect moment to come clean about the pregnancy test. And later on, when that no longer mattered, he had turned the tables and followed the path of least resistance.

Kate knew that it was time to get everything off her chest once and for all. And poor Maggie might just have to be her sounding board. Hopefully later on this evening. Before they both got too busy and before Kate lost her nerve.

But right now, all she wanted was to gather up her better self. To soak in the beauty that would have to sustain her until the next time. Because as Maggie had said, *there'd always be a next time!*

Kate snatched the phone from her purse and quickly ran a search of Rembrandt's later portraits. No more robes, only jackets in dark and sobering shades—he'd lost so much by then.

Kinda like the wardrobe of a sometimes-depressed divorcee?

Note to self—go shopping!

Scrutinize—to pore over—always finding something new or different.

Maybe so, she thought, looking at the portrait. Not this man. In a world forever changing, *her* Rembrandt would always be twenty-three, on the threshold of success, and bravely reaching for the stars.

"Look who's here, Samantha?"

No, no, no! Kate knew a lot about bumpy landings and was about to Google Rembrandt's downfall. But this unexpected intrusion meant that now she'd be forced to make polite conversation when all she really wanted to do was tell them to fuck off.

"Hi again; hope you're enjoying the Gardner." Kate swore she could hear her face crack.

"Better than the Tate," offered the man who on reflection, resembled an English politician with floppy blonde hair and an insipid complexion.

"Yes and no, darling," said Samantha as if to reinstate an absolute. Something Kate had imagined as they began what might turn into a parliamentary debate.

Kate rolled her eyes and gave up altogether, saying, "You'll have to excuse me; I'm off to see the tapestries next door."

Looking at their faces, she understood how odd she must seem to them. Avoidance, which had never been prominent in her personality, was front and center today. A need for privacy that bordered on rudeness.

But still…she looked to Rembrandt as if he knew what to do, and whispered, "Should I make a run for it?" Samantha, especially, represented women she'd met through Angus. The cocktail party wives who smiled with knives out and ate salads for lunch—without the dressing.

How could she possibly admit to someone like Samantha that she was no longer part of a couple—a question of marital status was bound to come up as long as there was a gentleman in the mix. It would be innocent enough: *have you and your husband lived here long?* And on it would go.

To Kate's way of thinking, women like Samantha would also make fun of her if they knew how much she had loved being married. Coupledom and the united front it represented had suited her personality right from the get-go. Samantha, on the other hand, appeared to be a woman who enjoyed the ornamental satisfaction of a mate. Kate had the common sense to understand that she was being a bit harsh, but how would Samantha's type respond if they knew that she and Angus had planned on renewing their vows on their twenty-fifth anniversary, which in hindsight seemed about as corny as Kansas in August.

The more she felt squeezed in, the more she sensed the proverbial coin toss: those silent attendees framed in gold versus the voices of a crowd that had begun to swell. The Brits and their irritating debate or the steady rise of her own self-confidence.

Maggie had been right; no woman should risk all for the sake of one man or make sacrifices just to be loved. And yet hadn't Kate done both.

She offered them a smile. But not really. Just two plumpish lines caught between childhood and maturity, and she fled.

And then, just as she reached the entrance to the Tapestry Room, Samantha's voice broke the silence, scratching like a bad conscience. Kate turned to look and then realized it had simply been the acoustics; the Brits were right where she'd left them.

Stepping into the room was like venturing into the past: carpets that would have been at home on the castle walls of old York. She was enveloped within the braided tapestries—a hushed haven—a room devoid of other voices. She had never been here with Angus.

This room was lonely with relief, something that today seemed like a gift rather than a burden. And it was perfectly set up for dancing. How odd, she thought; she had never tried to lure Angus to this particular gallery. The word sanctuary kept repeating itself. A gallery that presented a tranquil visage, and at the same time possessed a silence as familiar as the inside of a church.

She felt her body bending. Sensed her parents kneeling beside her, the smell of wood polish surrounding them as they did their duty within their small island church. She recalled the times she'd asked for forgiveness because she'd been about to break her father's heart in her desperation to leave Maine.

And after she'd dropped out of Boston College, she'd come in here to the Tapestry Room to dissemble her truths before laying it all out for him in person.

Standing here now, she pictured his face on the day she'd left the helm of the *Mary-Kate* for good. That final summer that she'd told him about the three-week pre-college course at MECA in Portland.

It was here in the quietude of this gallery that she'd mentally spelled out the reasons for all that leave-taking. And the jobs she'd gotten to support herself after that. And though he hadn't quite forgiven her, they were both content that dear Mary had died knowing that Kate had escaped the lure of the sea to follow her own dreams—her footfalls weighted by a packed suitcase were bound for Boston and a career in fine art. Instead of riding the high waves, she would paint the colors of the sea in whatever blue or green that would accommodate the atmospheric conditions. She would configure the outcroppings to suit her mood. At least that had been her desire.

She thought of her mum and all those prayers, her fear of the wildly robust storms like the one that had swallowed James Flannagan decades ago off Cape Elizabeth. There was rumor in that disappearance, an offbeat hint that he'd tried to kill himself because of Brigid, but that was long after she'd sat for a painting, and after Kate's father was in his teens.

She had followed her dreams and for a little while there was a peaceful coexistence of opinions in the Hull Island house, and when her path changed again, she'd been able to tell her father about the internship at the art gallery in a trendy part of Boston. And that even someone young and without art creds could be considered for what was essentially a handholding position, and that it was more about the hands she was expected to hold and the egos that needed to be salved and resalved. And she'd been quite good at it.

But the plum she had offered Tom Flannagan, was when the gallery owner asked her to become their ad hoc bookkeeper (it seemed that she had a reluctant flair for numbers), which meant a continuing salary with bonuses to stash away for the future. Back then, it was the most comforting concept of all, since she could take this sort of work with her wherever she might end up. No one would have guessed that she would end up quite close to where she'd started.

The Tapestry Room was the most silent of spaces, the best place to hold Kate's innermost thoughts and ambitions. And yet, there was one voice that could never be quelled, not even in here and that was the way her mother had talked about the rumor mill that prevented Kate's father from talking about his mother, Brigid. The buzz that surrounded young Tom Flannagan from living a normal childhood. All because of *Summer Dreams*, which she'd only just realized was the reason for his reluctance to talk about Brigid. To coin her mother's phrase: *those slights stayed with your dad all through his childhood, clung like a mean shadow wherever he went,* now made perfect sense.

Her father had lots of scars from his lobstering, but those beneath the surface must have hurt the most and yet he'd kept it all to himself.

Back then, she had stayed on in Boston and tried to become a better version of herself because of the pain that she'd caused by leaving. And then, what had originated as an inconsequential job became a stepping stone to a collaborative art group and a seat on their board of trustees.

There was more, of course, things she hadn't shared: the hours and hours spent after classes in the silent company of the Old Masters, and then the way those visits had become all about the improbable stranger with the deep blue eyes and their time in the Spanish Cloister. It had been pure *Kismet* and given his love for Mary and their own 'cute-meet', she now realized that her father would have understood.

But it had been the type of fate that for Kate, seemed to have walked off the pages of one of the romance novels she'd devoured into the dead of night when she couldn't sleep. A tied-in-a-bow rapture that people wrote about but that she never once believed could happen. That was what she'd experienced when she met Angus that first time.

Those were not things she'd cared to share with the man who'd had her baby shoes bronzed and still hadn't removed the stepstool she'd used on the *Mary-Kate* in order to reach the helm.

But those notions had been her ideal. A type of rapture she longed for Brigid to have known: an unfamiliar ownership of desire in its first blush. Even when things turn out badly.

Chapter 15

1936

Brigid smiled wistfully as she wrapped Tommy against a wind too sharp for such a picture-perfect day. "See all the boats out there," she said as she held him to the open window. "It's like a postcard."

"Boats!" Tommy shouted and wriggled to be free.

Pleasure boats and fishing boats cradled between uneven waves, all making way through the breakwater. The wind caught the sound of luffing sails. Rigging slapped the masts and boatmen struggled to take on their cargos.

The entire cast of characters played out against the bluest of blues. Then she thought of James and her mood turned again. When Tommy was all tucked up and ready to go, she put on her waders and a jacket that would need to come off by lunchtime. Once again, Helen had come to the rescue with the ease of someone who longed for children of her own.

Lifting Tommy into her arms, Brigid said, "We're going to visit auntie Helen."

"Cat," Tommy said, tilting his little head as he pointed into the distance. He truly was her beating heart and the sustenance of her soul. Today as so many other times, she wanted to whisk him away from the village that because of his father, she had yet to call home.

Instead, they were just taking a short walk to the Budreau house down the hill. "Let's go, little man."

"Hi Tommy boy!" Helen reached for him through the doorway wearing another of the plaid shirts that her brother had left behind.

"He's getting heavy, but we couldn't wait to get out and see you, right Tommy, and there's auntie Helen's cat," Brigid said.

"Look, Tommy, over in the corner. Why don't I just set you down on the floor there next to Rascal and you and he can have a nice chat."

"You really have a way with kids."

"Comes from taking care of my brother and now Mom isn't much of a grownup herself, and she complains louder than any toddler."

Brigid could hear muttering behind the semi-closed door off the kitchen. A thwack followed, and Helen jumped up to see what had happened. She turned toward Brigid and said, "Don't mind her; she's just letting me know that she knows we have company."

Brigid walked over and poked her head in the door, and said, "Morning Mrs. Budreau."

"She won't say much."

"She looks pretty good this morning."

"Pretty as a picture, I tried to tell her," Helen said half in and half out of the doorway. "And speaking of pictures...there's a painter wandering around here, or so our friendly postmaster said."

"You thinking of having your house painted?" Brigid said as she removed her coat.

"No, silly." Helen brought cups to the table and poured their coffee, saying. "Sit down and I'll tell you.

"Luke says he's Italian and paints portraits and maybe seascapes. But you know Luke."

"Did he mention what this *Eyetalian's* name is or anything more enlightening or did he just stop right there like he always does and leave you wondering?"

"I pried it out of him…Giacomo Canelli, but he likes people to call him Jake."

"I don't suppose this Jake has anything to do with the way you've done your hair?"

"Maybe I'm just experimenting."

"Is there anymore you'd like to tell me?"

"Okay…Luke puffed himself up like he understood all about art, said the man was asking about the Town Hall supper that's posted on the board. Said he was thinking of recruiting people to sit for him. And I thought since James was away, you and I could take Tommy."

"Gee, I'll just check my calendar," Brigid said as she flipped through an imaginary page. "Yep, we're free that night."

"Hear that, Tommy? We're going out Friday night and have us some biscuits and stew and apple pie."

Brigid watched as her little boy gazed adoringly at the cat, his tiny hand patting Rascal's lion-like head. If only James wasn't such a curmudgeon, she'd get one of their own.

"Nothing is going to matter as long as Rascal's in the picture."

And by the time they'd made their plan for Friday night, both Tommy and Rascal were asleep on the floor and emitting soft little wheezes of contentment into the air.

Chapter 16

2018

Kate walked across the floor of the Tapestry Room and set her right hand on the top of the piano. It was polished and strangely warm as if the notes of a love song had only recently been played. Maggie's brother played. She had said that she wanted Kate to meet him, but then she'd said a lot to entice Kate into dating. She lifted her hand from the surface and tried to imagine what Paul would look like. Would he be as nice and as much fun as Maggie, or would he just be another divorced person looking for someone to fill in the days and nights. Because that's what dating seemed to insinuate at this stage in her life. And the idea of dating Maggie's older brother was in complete contrast with Maggie who had suddenly decided that she wanted to date a much younger man. *Cougar,* is what she'd said over the phone. Maggie had declared that she was 'tired of and bored with' the usual crop of single men. How then, could Kate refute a friend's obvious skills at online dating, and especially one who was willing to share said skills with her dearest friend. She supposed she couldn't.

What would Maggie say if she were here right now, besides regaling the attributes of her brother? Would she expect Kate to admit to a need for more time to sort and sift and categorize her very trying emotions. Like she'd been doing from the moment she'd arrived at the museum.

Or would Maggie say that Kate was spending far too much time with dead people when she should be out partying and trying on new clothes and trying out new hairdos.

Angus had loved her in black, just like he'd loved so many things back then. Like the way she had begged him beneath heavily mascaraed eyelashes to turn away from *El Jaleo* and notice her instead.

Kate pictured Maggie—shiny hair hiding her face as she tipped her head and scanned the inventory of men on the new dating app that she'd only just found. It was a remodeled version of the usual catalog of available men. The headings that were adapted for the silver haired crowd or like-minded creatives. There were apps for the faith-based groups, and even one for those who belonged to Mensa. A plethora of available men that Kate found too much to take in without a playbook or at least written instructions.

But Maggie's drive, this idea of finding someone young enough to turn heads, and yet old enough to appreciate the finer points of romance, was even more complex to understand. Unless, and what Kate surmised to be true, it had a great deal to do with the struggle to find someone who would be a stand-in, albeit a poor one, for Maggie's first husband, Edward.

Maggie had always been adept at crisis management, and was able to maintain her positive attitude with or without dating, but there was still a hole in her heart.

While Kate wanted to give in, she questioned the mirrors that offered a familial glimpse of the descendent with dark curls and eyes the color of bluebells. And the self-doubt and a sadness that had permeated the Flannagan household.

Kate recalled Maggie's follow-up edict: *you're suffering from the blues or the blahs or whatever; but you are not dead!*

Kate looked down at herself, the slight bulk, the lack of color, the pattern of aging that had come up out of nowhere. And she silently vowed to find the woman who had marched alongside other women, who'd forged bonds of solidarity when times presented themselves. And as far as she was concerned, there'd be no more begging for any attention of any kind ever again.

Given her druthers, she would always prefer the type of 'dancing' she and Angus had shared no matter the way their relationship had ended. A dance that was intense and complicated and borne out of dreams that no one else knew.

Love that later became wrapped in the sound of castanets and the strumming of a guitar that always harkened back to the romance of Spain.

Fusions, like mixed media, until the last page and the last line—the end. Where it's 2018 and she's finally found herself.

Or could this possibly be the beginning. The first day of the rest of her life—a feeling that might be harder to extract from the previous years. But then maybe she wouldn't need to. After all, wasn't this about growth and maturity.

And then, she heard that unmistakable grating voice, only to find a flash of red (or was it really a deep orange) when she turned around.

Kate made it back to the Dutch Room with the agility of a truant avoiding the coppers. Rembrandt and his nondescript eyes appeared as though he'd been expecting the sound of her changing emotions. Something akin to the blue-greens of the sea. Could he hear the metronome of her steps, or feel the verbal caresses she'd tossed his way, she wondered, and realized how truly exhausted she was. And how her emotions were getting the best of her and all the while she believed that she'd begun to cope.

A flush rose up from her neck. Trying to take her mind off the heat, she reached for her phone and texted Maggie, inviting her for a drink later on. There was so much to tell, even a forgotten punchline to the story on the day that she'd found out that Angus had been cheating.

The clacking of her heels had triggered the memory of the way his loafers had landed in a pile. The day she'd tossed his sorry ass out the door. Before she headed home to Maine.

Kate texted Maggie again, this time she turned her back on Rembrandt to shield him from a comical meme that referenced the male anatomy (in honor of her mother).

She then added-in a smiley face for good measure.

Maggie immediately texted back a question mark, which then required another explanation.

The messages went back and forth for a few moments, until she finally assured Maggie that instead of beating up on herself all morning, she had been scoping out the museum for available men. What Kate left out was the fact that she thought they'd be more suitable for Maggie, but that would come later.

What's a little white lie in desperate situations, Kate thought as the hard-earned parentheses framing her mouth suddenly mirrored a happy emoji.

And when she looked up, the gallery had suddenly sprung to life.

A beehive of whispers—small boys trailing on the heels of a woman with ginger hair who was holding up a printed sign. *How cute are they!* It occurred to Kate that this could have easily been a scene from a Norman Rockwell poster, right down to the apple cheeks and matching school sweaters.

Though the young woman leading them was stoic enough, and was far younger than the museum guides, no one could have been prepared for what appeared to be a mutiny in the making: two of the ginger-haired boys broke rank as if a starter pistol had been discharged.

Then, with their small fists in battle mode, they headed straight for the righteously armored Earl of Arundel, hanging on the wall just to Kate's left.

Everything happened so fast; Kate felt a swish of material as one of the escaping boys slid by her. He shouted just above a whisper, "Back off O'Brien."

"You back off, Smitty," said the other escapee as he punched young O'Brien in the shoulder.

"Stop!" Kate swung around, as if the edict had sprung from her instead of the young woman who on reflection looked to be thin enough to be blown over at a windy intersection. Kate had no authority here, but she detested bad behavior in public places.

As a teenager, she'd been in demand for babysitting jobs. And while she'd made good money, the whole experience had refueled her desire to become an artist instead of a stay-at-home mom like tiny Mary Flannagan. And no matter how their parents gushed, or how adorable those little chubby cheeked babies and runny-nosed toddlers were, Kate had never changed her mind.

She finally lifted her shoulders and all sixty-six inches of her rose up to model her thoughts. Then, she strode over to join the red-faced young woman. "These two yours?" Kate said.

"Are you kidding, I'm only a sub who stupidly volunteered so their class wouldn't lose this field trip."

"At least they've listened to you," Kate said, as she shot a stony look at the boys whose cheeks had gone from apple red to a full-on facial glow.

"You don't understand…we have four more galleries to go through; I'm never going to last the day!"

Just then, something clanged. The young woman swiveled, her voice a strangled scream. "Don't you dare touch that, Richie, or you'll be in detention for a week!"

Kate stood her ground; the little wannabe heroes with their alter-egos running amuck were herded back into a predictable line. Her own hero was safe from the chocolate stains that were now evident on tiny hands. The twenty-somethings with their skinny jeans and Boston College sweatshirts had come and gone. Quite suddenly, Kate sensed an urgency to return home to the little house in Maine.

More than likely, it wouldn't be a forever home, but at least the new bed was not large enough to imagine a life vibrant with disappointment—lovemaking aside. And as the fates would have it, there had been a timely spread in one of the magazines at the salon in Brunswick where she went when her hair needed taming. And when those same fates intervened again, she was face-to-face with a familiar Mainer who, when young, had spent time repainting the scarred clapboards on the Flannagan house.

He now managed the paint department at the area hardware store. So, with a little color and a bit of fabric, and enticed by the purity of white, she had created an oasis as soft and quiet as snow in a thick forest. An analogy she'd kept to herself while he mixed the various droplets from the dispenser, attached a label, and then handed over the finished product.

She was about to leave when he put the same hand on her back that he'd once used to throw the winning pitches for their high school team. Grinning as broadly as she remembered, he gently prodded her toward the door. "It's called Snow," Kate.

Later on, when normal energy returned to her body, and with the bedroom makeover nearly finished, she'd gone on the hunt for something blue. And as with the paint, she'd found the exact shade in prints of *Girl with the Pearl Earring* in a gift shop on Maine Street in Brunswick. Her cup had begun to fill without exactly overflowing, but time would tell.

And then. Nothing but long bouts of loneliness, and the times when she could barely get out of bed. Days when she could only go as far as the shoreline to stare at an ocean always in flux.

Every day there, she'd bow her head to the infinite possibilities that lay beyond the horizon. And she would think of the Angus she had trusted—stretched out on that oversized sofa nursing a glass of scotch. Sharing his day.

Or straight out of the shower, glistening with want and drawing her into his arms.

Time and again, the ocean would lull her into believing she could start over, meet someone who would fully appreciate her, even though she'd grown prickly in her confinement.

She'd groped through the shadows to find the sunshine. And followed it wherever it landed on her walls. And she'd pull at the drapes that bracketed the windows that allowed the sun to fire her flesh and open up those old wounds.

That's when Angus would reach out as if he had a specific antenna trained on her emotions. He would throw her off balance each and every time. Were they destined to fail given their age difference, as Moses had intimated? Or maybe like her, Angus simply didn't know how to let go.

And now he was doing it again with messages that contained some unexpected and bittersweet recognition of regret.

Just three days ago, he'd left a message hinting that they should try again—of course he was older—but infinitely wiser? It didn't fly. Those were the words she thought too shameless to share with anyone. Until now. Maggie had managed to find the crack in all of Kate's best intentions and she would get another earful tonight, Kate thought.

Their friendship made her realize that because of life with Angus, she could count her female friends on one hand and none really close. But this newer version of a friendship at such an important juncture in her life had all the makings of one that no matter what, would go on into old age.

Kate had known women who had nothing to offer but watered-down pablum. Not exactly a remedy to those struggling with divorce or weight or even someone rounding on fifty. But not Maggie. She went after what was there for the asking and made sure that her friends would have the confidence to do the same.

"At least she's moved on," Kate whispered into air that still held the whorl of childish chaos. Maggie had been quite well off when Edward died; she was still young and beautiful though incredibly lonely. Husband number two had come along during that vulnerable time and syphoned off half of that inherited wealth, and still she remained optimistic. When they met, the two women realized they lived close to Cape End; Kate in a remodeled rental and Maggy in a neatly packaged cottage nestled into impenetrable hedges of pink beach roses, but even closer to the sea.

Until she moved back, Kate hadn't realized just how much she'd missed that location. There was a season and a rhythm to everything: residents enjoyed their solidarity during the off-season—the icy glare of sun on the rocks, leaves turning ahead of the arrival of strangers to their shore.

Visitors flocked from far and wide to watch the sky slip the hem of dark blue water during the warm summer months.

They stood shoulder to shoulder and balanced the uneven boulders in order to admire the bottle green glitter of incoming waves or watch whole squadrons of gulls minding everyone's business as they wheeled overhead in search of food.

Summertime at Cove's End was about streets filled with the sounds of laughter and joy that on occasion must compete with the roar of shiny motorcycles.

And sand toys and sailboats get to bob in unison during interludes of antique cars and holiday campers as they parade the smallish roads at their own peril. Many will return to buy property and place their mark on a coast they've come to love.

Kate's mind also reeled as she fused all the alternating memories. There was no good way to order this new life, except by living it. She looked at Rembrandt one last time; he knew her truths. And through it all, he never changed his inscrutable expression. *Not for applause or fame or even for the young bride he'd loved and lost.*

Tossing him a cagy wink, and with her best museum voice, she said, "I'll be back—but definitely on a different date."

Chapter 17

1936

Dear Diary,

 Helen and I went to the Town Hall dinner as planned, but it didn't turn out the way I thought it might, not that I'd been out much since I got married. But Helen kept watching the door and I watched her and wondered why she hadn't bothered with her usual comments about Mrs. Hough's putting on weight or Mr. Manson's needing new teeth. And then, I knew the answer: the man whose presence had suddenly filled the doorway. Heads had turned, mind you, really swiveled when he coughed loudly, and I immediately understood why she'd been so keen on meeting him. He was handsome in an unusual way, darker complected and somewhat exotic, at least that's my first impression. He carried himself with the air of a man used to attention. Not like the way James acted when he wanted my attention, but this Jake person really seemed to think he was special. And maybe he is.

 Helen had even shoved her elbow into my ribs and someone seated on the other side of her had actually gasped. The painter's entrance was dramatic enough, but he was backlit by the setting sun and the effect was stunning.

 And then, the oddest thing. Helen shot out of her seat and walked over and introduced herself. More heads had turned, but why had I felt so left out? She's single and being a model for one of his paintings was all she'd talked since I'd taken Tommy for a visit.

 Was I jealous? If James ever heard what happened and the way Helen had invited the stranger to sit at our table, he would lock me in the house.

Brigid heard the knock and put down the pen and put a dishtowel over the diary. Then, she went to the door with Tommy on her heels.

"Are you still talking to me?" Helen said.

"Tommy, tell auntie Helen hello and then go play in the parlor, please."

"That's not good."

"What do you want me to say...you were so rude and it's taken you three days to come see me."

"He wants me—us—to model for him."

"Have you been taking your mum's medication? Or do you think the gossips will just cover their eyes and ears and not whisper a thing afterward?"

"It's not *that* bad; just a few of what he called preliminary sketches, and then, maybe once or twice more when he finds the right place to have us sit for him."

"There won't be any *us*, Helen; James would kill me!"

"He doesn't have to know, does he?" Helen said. "After all, he's usually gone for three weeks at a time."

"I don't know how he wouldn't find out the minute he's home, and I can't risk that."

"Jake is down at the dock scouting out locations now, and James wouldn't bother himself with an Italian; you know how he is about foreigners."

"Listen to you and all that artsy stuff...locations, indeed."

But of course, they'd gone down to the docks to have a look, Tommy between them, happy just to be near the boats. Brigid spotted Jake (no one else had a wooden easel or wore what looked like a doctor's coat with paint stains on it) and this man's arm was extended and his brush was angled as if he was searching for something beyond. His back was straining the fabric of his jacket and his legs were sturdy and slightly apart, balanced, as the water sloshed beneath the float.

"Isn't it exciting?" Helen exclaimed.

"If you say so, but I still don't understand what this has to do with me," Brigid said. "And before you go into a lengthy explanation, be mindful of small ears."

"Got it," Helen said. Then she beamed at Tommy and spelled out the important parts. "Just think of the fun this could be, think of it as a H-O-L-I-D-A-Y while I watch the little man when it's your turn to M-O-D-E-L.

"Good lord, Helen! Can you really imagine me being *alone* with him," she whispered.

"I'd rather not, but it's the only way this could work since he's already discovered that we're good friends and has seen the two of us out and about…remember that day we took little man out for ice cream."

Helen had forgotten to spell the one thing that Tommy picked up on. And all of a sudden, he was tugging at her skirt. "I guess I've gone and done it now, right Brigid?"

"Thanks a bunch," Brigid said as she watched Helen lift Tommy onto her hip.

Chapter 18

2018

Kate's attachment to the Gardner was on par with the way she'd become attached to Boston. Once she'd swallowed the lump in her throat and walked away from the college of her dreams, she'd actually found joy in learning a new job—even the hand-holding that hadn't been fully explained. Like coaxing one of the painters from his lair after a bad review. Or minding a cat while the paint dried on an artist's last-minute entry—said cat having had an affinity for sable brushes. The bookkeeping took a little more effort; numbers didn't pop off the page the way paint colors had, but she had mastered that too. And as luck would have it, there was an opening at a family run accounting firm in Brunswick when it became necessary to return to Maine. The offices were set up in their home, which while not a period style, was still pleasantly old-fashioned, just like the homeowners themselves.

The desk they'd provided for Kate's office had displaced everything except the heart and soul of the firm. The scent of old age crept from a metal filing cabinet, folders overflowed with past accounts, leaving very little room for the new ones Kate hoped to bring in.

Juxtaposed within such ordinariness, was the seasonal greenery and a tree heavily laden with deep pink blossoms that were visible through the one and only window.

Kate had brought her own calculator and sharp pencils. And a worn but not masculine briefcase that she hoped would make her appear legitimate enough to handle the needs of those who simply couldn't deal with numbers on any level.

Clients walking into her tiny cubicle would squeeze into an armchair angled in order to provide a clear view of Kate's favorite photos: a scene taken after a storm that had whipped through Cape End. And a small depiction of Vermeer's *The Concert*. The mementos always caught the attention of fidgeters and gave them a topic besides taxes to discuss. And gave her a chance to blather on about the Gardner until someone politely yawned.

Thankfully, besides men, Maggie had long been interested in art and loved museum hopping, and when she wasn't volunteering her time at the animal shelter or with activists working on projects close to her heart, she could be found at the Farnsworth Museum in Rockland, Maine. Kate had nearly crashed into a painting to avoid bumping into Maggie the day they'd met because Maggie's eyes had been focused on one of the male docents. For Kate, the experience, except for making a new friend, hadn't been anything like the one in Boston.

The Gardner Museum was not to be fast-tracked in a day, sampling a little of this or a little of that, like canapes at a party.

Here—as she'd just reaffirmed—one made careful selections and feasted on a menu from far-away lands until they were full to bursting. And then, when the hunger became impossible to ignore, came back again, finding new rooms in which to satisfy their cravings.

Her personal wish-list had been banqueting at one of the long tables with guest artists from the past. In her mind, the table from the Dutch Room was already set and Rembrandt and Johannes were bookended while she basked in their presence.

That little fabrication was one of the few things she had shared with anyone who would listen. What she hadn't shared was that food had more recently become a foe hiding in the kitchen cupboard or beneath loose clothing.

Kate tugged at her blouse with a new determination. She supposed there must be a way to make friends with the foods she loved. But as with the man with the baggy jeans, she wanted another s*igne.* Like in a once enjoyed Italian movie when bird droppings stood for good luck. Something to prove that just like the house that had been for sale in that movie, this hapless eating out of heartbreak wasn't intended to be her *destino.*

The Irish had their superstitions all mapped out too, and both cultures loved their bread and potatoes. Bacon and spudless stews were a good possibility now that dieting had taken on new twists and turns, though she couldn't quite get the hang of imaginary meats. Did she even stand a chance, she wondered, as once again, hunger beckoned.

Then, as she made her way back to the stairs, there was another scent, far removed from anything to do with food. She had completely forgotten about her favorite window — where earlier, the museum employee had been crouching. It was her own 'Juliet' moment, a time to peek at the gardens below, take in the scent of whatever flowers were in season. Be surprised by the nasturtiums as if she'd never seen them before. And out of nowhere, the idea that the balconies had come about after one of Isabella's trips to Italy. Perhaps gazing from a window in the *sala* of a favorite palazzo. Had she, like Kate leaned out over a unique landscape or water glistening in a nearby canal. Had Isabella brought that idea home to roost here at the Gardner, or was it just a coincidence.

The garden was filled with female statuary and today, it reminded Kate of a stage set as if she and Angus were once again on holiday: Altos de Chavon in the Dominican Republic. Angus had taken her away for their wedding anniversary and they'd reveled in the sun and surf and marveled at the handcrafted stone amphitheater right out of the likes of Hollywood and had once hosted Frank Sinatra. The small elevated village was the best place to buy amber jewelry, which Angus had mistakenly thought represented the fourth year of marriage. The sun had devoured them and turned their skin to the same shade of burned butter and they'd returned to Boston renewed. But in a moment of disgust, she had taken the lovely gold studded orbs and their small presentation pouch and tossed them in the trash on her way out of Boston to start over again.

Peering down, Kate inhaled the essence from today's selection of flowers; she considered the people who emerged from the walkways looking much like pieces on a game board. Without so much as a nod, the various participants suddenly moved a few paces to their right, each taking a moment to consider the bust of Medusa. And the columns and the breathtaking whites and greens that popped against such a bland sky. As Kate leaned out, she spotted what appeared to be blue cineraria in the foreground, and then, one of the players turned around and her heart pinched again. If possible, she would have made this her screensaver. Instead of a homely patchwork garden, Mary Flannagan's look-alike was bent over a border of tall blue flowers much the same way her mother would in order to admire the lush lilac blossoms that grew near their back door. The memory was strong enough to make Kate's nose twitch with latent allergies. But before she had time to blink, a new player with longish dark hair that curled over the collar of a blue long-sleeved sweater had moved into that space and changed the game board again. He turned. Almost as if he'd felt her eyes bearing down. And like the man with the wrong gait that she'd seen earlier, it wasn't Angus. But had she wanted it to be him reaching out to her from somewhere inside the museum? This time the ache in her chest was quite different. This time she worried: emotional clocks weren't meant to be turned back with the seasons. There was no saving grace to be gotten from an extra hour of heartache. As far as she could tell, nothing to be gained from forgiving and forgetting either. And yet she wondered: would it have mattered if they'd spent more time on Hull Island, maybe even delved into the mystery of her grandmother's life — a shared project to pull them in tight. Anything to take his mind off whatever he'd been doing with *the other woman.*

Kate frowned; how could she have considered that he might want to spend more time on Hull Island. He'd scoffed at too many things that were important to her back then, things that she hadn't realized were part and parcel of his new relationship. And now, she was quite certain that he would do the same with or without that other woman.

Looking down at this long-haired stranger, it was easy to recall those few visits to the Flannagan homestead. And how her father had maintained that the third floor was off limits each time with excuses: needed repairs—his overprotectiveness about the condition of the stairs; the walls still wet with primer—he was going to make that space into his personal workshop.

But in essence Tom Flannagan was not so much trying to cover the hard-to-remove paint or the stink of turpentine. It would have been his continual attempt to free the room of the scent of guilty pleasures that no one dared talk about.

But what happens if Angus really does want you back?

She was beginning to yoyo emotionally. Pros and cons and remembered slights—moments of uplifting joy. Nothing that would do her any good except to drain her of the last of her energy.

The early morning train, the unshakable reminder of the museum theft, the hours wading through nostalgia and all for what? *Do yourself a favor and skip the Short Gallery; Isabella won't know the difference*—the times Kate had virtually genuflected in front of the portrayal of her by Mower. Isabella was dressed in black—formidable—but she's also holding a red-covered book. Again, that spot of color to draw the eye.

Walking on, Kate considered the copers of life. Someone very like Isabella. Someone to emulate. And another moment in which Kate wished she were a writer.

Maybe a novel about politics; they seem to do well. Except Kate couldn't bear the thought of incurring more wrath from her resolute conservative-thinking father.

And Angus; he leaned so far left she always feared he'd fall over and break something.

And honestly, how could one write a scintillating story about an independent?

Maybe she would simply buy a book instead. Something to read on the train ride home or just add to her collection of gardening books.

She hurried down the stairs and beelined toward the small cornucopia of gifts and books in the museum shop. But as soon as she reached the doorway, she had to stop in order to remove her shawl.

Discretely turning to one side, she unbuttoned the top two buttons of her blouse—it wasn't uncommon to go from zero to hot in sixty seconds these days. Not unlike a Ferrari but with far less glamor.

Once inside, she spotted a brand of tea her father truly liked. A good *signe:* the cannister was labeled 'the Ruckus'. Her main hope was that the funny label would amuse him and relax him into wanting to talk about the photograph. And maybe he'd talk about Brigid.

It was the best possible outcome, she thought as she slid past a woman who was wrangling two large shopping bags from her arms and was trying to leave the shop with as much grace and as little breakage as possible.

Then it was Kate's turn at being graceful. She spotted a rump wearing bagging jeans, and immediately recognized the man who was bent over and trying not to lean on the glass case.

As and as soon as she reached the book section, she discretely fanned herself with the edge of her blouse, and as she turned, her eyes landed on a guidebook of color coding. *To buy or not to buy*, she thought and would a book like this prompt her back into painting.

There wasn't anything on indoor gardening; not that she needed any more books at all, but it would have been preferable to all the others, at least for today. Her eyes roamed the shelves and counters and she spotted something that might be the best solution: a scarf that was part of a collective produced by the Gardner's challenge. Artists' designs that were based on the courtyard blossoms. In the end, Kate decided on a longish scarf in a blue and magenta print, which would be a definite enhancement to her disastrous wardrobe rut. Just about anything would, she thought, suddenly sensing she was being watched. And she was. By the salesgirl standing behind the check-out counter.

As soon as she understood why, Kate offered what her father called her Shirley Temple smile. Then she took the cannister she had unwittingly put into the hand she'd draped with the pashmina, into her exposed hand.

The girl nodded, which made Kate feel like she was twelve. But then Kate studied her the way she might have one of the studio models at BC. She must have been twenty-something; definitely slimmed by a striking tailored gray wool jacket and to Kate's envy, pin-straight hair in a light brown shade. And tiny silver eyebrow rings.

And beyond all of that, was the salesgirl's air of efficiency and even maturity. But her pallor distracted from her prettiness. And was distinctly different from Kate's hot pink cheeks, and she wondered if the salesgirl was also suffering from a case of the blahs.

She quickly picked out a pair of summery earrings for Maggie's upcoming birthday and she walked over and put all her items on the counter, placing the scarf up for inspection, saying, "I wanted a book on gardening, but I settled for this instead."

"I think I can find you one if you like."

Within a few moments, Kate had just what she wanted and then some. And as her purchases were being tabulated, Kate was imagining her next credit card bill, but also wondering if those eyebrow rings hurt when provoked by normal expressions.

Kate may have conversed with ghostly scholars and Renaissance painters as well as her dear departed mother, but she would carry this small interaction with her as the perfect ending to her first morning back at the Gardner. And at the same time, she silently vowed that she would never ever attach anything anywhere on her face!

Other shoppers picked up on her mood and smiled as they passed. Kate's facial muscles hadn't had this much of a workout in months. And neither had her wallet.

She quickly grabbed a brochure for Maggie, and tossed it in with the other items and jauntily swung past the fresh batch of incoming shoppers. The phrase 'happy camper' came to mind. And once again, the word *signe* as she spotted the tall man from the courtyard who was heading her way.

She ducked her head. And, carelessly slammed into the exit door. The bag hit the floor.

"Let me help."

Kate looked up. She'd never thought of a man as beautiful, but his face was perfectly symmetrical. Like a model for a Polo ad or maybe for a painting, which was the most bizarre thought she'd had all day, but she said, "Thanks...that was pretty careless of me."

"Hope there's nothing breakable."

"No, a can of tea and a book and oh well, it doesn't really matter," she stammered suddenly as shy as a young filly.

"Didn't I see you earlier?"

Kate looked into his eyes. They were blue, though not the same blue as her ex-husband's. *His* held the depth of an ocean that begged for a swim. The type where a woman might end up drowning from sorrow if she wasn't careful.

This man's eyes had the quality of fading chambray. Less threatening. And suddenly quite appealing. And though she hadn't exerted their power in quite a while, she reverted to her dimples for a second time, and said, "I don't think so, but thanks again for the assist."

"Don't mention it...my name's Ross, just in case we run into each other again."

"I'm Kate," she offered because of the way his lips had curved when he stood by to let her pass. Then she realized he was actually flirting with her and it wasn't at all unpleasant, just unfamiliar.

"Here...take my card, please."

She teetered on the brink of things she couldn't say, so instead, she took the card and offered a halfhearted smile. "I have to run or I'll miss my train."

And with a nod, she escaped through the door and back into the gray that hadn't changed an iota since she'd left home that morning.

Chapter 19

1936

Dear Diary,

I've stayed away from writing for too long, I know, but Helen came up with a plan that took me quite a while to digest. I'm still not certain I have because it involves Jake, or should I say my involvement with the artist because she's convinced me to sit for him. I'm still trying to talk myself into such a hairbrained idea, but she came by this afternoon for a picnic with me and Tommy. Then, as she had planned, Helen took Tommy to her house to play with the cat so that he would nap without a fuss. Then Jake arrived. Also, the way she'd planned. And now that he's left, I'm a total mess and not at all sure of how I feel about any of it.

I had food left and of course I offered him some, and he'd brought wine, which I'm not very knowledgeable about, but it was delicious. And it did put some color in my cheeks or so he said, but I felt the warmth spreading all over my body, which I didn't tell him. He told me a little about himself, how he had a friend who had a boat slip in the harbor for the summer months, and had let him stay in exchange for a painting of that boat, which is a pretty little thing that I'd seen on my walks with Tommy. Jake talked of many things, not at all shy about his accent or needing to be helped along with some of the island pronunciations and even my name, which came out sounding like Briggeete. As soon as we'd had a glass of the wine, I got up to clear away the food before the ants converged. He had good manners at least and picked up the leftover potato salad and Tommy's small glass, which meant that he had to follow me to the kitchen. Thankfully, the door is at the backside of the house and out of sight. Even with James off again, it was a terrible risk to be taking.

And then, Jake did the unthinkable; he put his hands on my shoulders and turned me from the sink and said he needed to study my face in the light from the window. He turned me around once and then he pulled me to him. I still don't know how it happened, but I know that I melted into his chest. It was the first time I'd felt my heart swell up from a man's touch, except for Tim of course, but even then, I'd been able to keep him from going further. I don't even know this stranger from away, but already, I'm not sure I can keep him at bay—he's electrifying. At least I made him leave as soon as he released his grip, but I don't know what if anything I can tell Helen, and I know she'll ask. Just like I know how much she's taken by him.

Chapter 20

2018

Kate had barely stepped off the train when a swirl of dirt caught in a small funnel of wind came up off the pavement. Someone behind her yelped, and a car door slammed, and a dog began to bark. Shielding her eyes, she turned. The Inn at Brunswick Station loomed like an abstract against a cremated sky. Right about now, guests would be perusing their menus or cozied up inside the bar area selecting a cocktail, and if she didn't live an hour away, she would settle for whatever therapy could be found inside a chilled martini glass along with a long hot bath. And just like that, a splat of icy rain hit her cheek. This, as Mary Flannagan would have said, was another example of Maine's wintry soul having a go at Mother Nature—even when the calendar put up a good fight.

Kate nestled into the folds of her shawl. And clutching the bag with all her goodies hard against her chest, she made a dash for the dented green Subaru that had belonged to her father. It was old, but reliable. A lot like the man. And both still had some mileage left. She sneezed. Today was a teaser: a fake spring day that might or might not go on for weeks. The weather laid further claim to her hair. But just in case she needed a reminder, another splat of cold water found its mark and dribbled onto the rolled edge of the shawl, and down inside the back of her blouse while she continued to search for her keys. Shivering—the exact opposite of those earlier flushes—she snatched open the door, tossed the bag across to the passenger seat, and dipped in behind the wheel. The engine sprung to life and as she waited for the heater to do the same, she was struck by what she'd done—another book to add to an already obscene number.

She had become an unintentional collector. Like being an accidental gardener, which is sort of the way she'd managed when she decided to go beyond the initial edge of her rental property, the place where landscaping met mossy wilderness.

There'd been times when she'd purchased books to avoid cake. Or housework. Or people in general. Things just happened and now she owned fiction by authors who offered the much-needed summer escape after a winter siege.

And pull-you-in-under-the-cover novels of crime and punishment from the outer islands to the streets of Portland and back along Maine's long coastline and even in the town where she now worked for a well-meaning couple nearing retirement.

Books that seemed to feed her soul as well as her appetite.

"It's really time to set some limits," she said as she leaned in to wipe the steam from the glass. And as she pulled out of the lot, a sound—not quite nails on a chalkboard—whipped back and forth and grated on her nerves as she realized it was just another thing to add to her to-do list.

Off to her left, the college campus was all but invisible behind what had quickly become a heavy curtain of rain. The solid architectural forms were always a constant reminder of her father's disappointment not only when she left the family business, but when she'd chosen Boston over Bowdoin. *How often can you ask for absolution?* Kate tapped the brakes and kept her eyes peeled for anyone trying to cross over to the buildings used for student housing. Each time she passed this stretch of road, her thoughts wandered back to those first days in Boston—not only all the brick, but the interesting students from near and far, and first impressions of both. Hours and hours had been spent assessing how different her life would become once she left the bosom of the ever-changing sea. God's work of art, her mother had claimed, but it had also been responsible for feeding the Flannagan clan in every way possible for decades.

Memories flooded in on the back side of the rain: dawn breaking—her father taking the *Mary-Kate* on a slow dance around the buoys he'd painted in yellow and black like bees, which Kate adored; the surge of a rebuilt engine as they headed toward deep water; his insistence that she take the helm; the knowledge that she would leave Maine and all of that behind, and break his heart.

Suddenly she swerved to avoid a pedestrian who hadn't used the crosswalk; she braked so hard that her tires hiccupped against the blacktop. And within moments, she had to swerve again as she'd nearly missed the road that led to the cottage that she'd begun to call home. Magically, it had been set among a row of thinning pines with natural paths that wound through the wood, and connected with other paths and other houses along that road. She pulled in beside the back door entrance knowing that tonight the wind would be too strong to notice the ocean breeze that sometimes graced her cottage.

It was different and yet gratifying to experience this change in the way she now lived her life, even though music and books were still a big part of daily living. Importantly, there was an element of healing in the quietude. In the ability to use nature as her backdrop instead of brick and mortar.

By the first of May, small harems of pink lady slippers would appear in a linear fashion show just beyond the large living room window. Then, they would find their way onto the shaded path behind the house and into the low-hanging boughs of the trees to hide, as if they'd already tired of nature's runway.

And before the summer heat arrived, the yard would be filled with yellow daffs, wild geraniums and ferns. Purple verge until all the bushes that surrounded the two birdbaths turned a fiery red. And she would be stuck trying to identify the shade that played tricks with the sun. And by then, all the neighborhood would rush to compete in this panoply of color. And yet, this was only the beginning of that extraordinary season; spring had only just begun and now as she turned off the engine, she realized that the rain had slowed but not enough to erase the bone chilling damp that would envelope her the moment she set foot outside the car.

She reached for her package, a solid reminder of the small literary obstacle course that was waiting for her inside, some of it still on the floor where she'd left them the night before. There were already shelves groaning under the weight of her collection, and like some crazed woman, she was about to add a new one, she thought as her foot hit the ground.

Beads of water spring-boarded off her hair and she dashed toward the covered doorway and immediately remembered the alarm system. She smiled in spite of herself as she remembered her faux pas. *"C'est la vie,"* she muttered as she entered what had to get by as a mud room for lack of a better word.

The scent of her damp shawl comingled with the smell of yesterday's meatloaf, burned-down incense, and fresh paint— the boldest of colors she'd recently used for the kitchen. As soon as she switched on the light, creamy yellow saffron tones lit the walls and bounced off the blue painted chairs.

There'd been so much residual sadness after leaving Boston, that she'd not only painted, but filled the cottage with an eclectic mix of old and new and somewhere in between. They were all appealing; most of them found at the flea market out on Route 1 near Wiscasset. And it made her feel better knowing they'd been loved by another Maine resident before being given a second chance.

Her imagination had blossomed in this back hallway, though: a forlorn little chair that might have been the subject of a Wyeth painting; a wooden coat rack meant for a family of ten; a tin-framed mirror from that long-ago trip to the Dominican Republic—and too unique to toss out with the discarded earrings.

Her reflection in the oval glass that was mounted next to the door was that of a wan and bedraggled woman who worried too much. For years after her mother died of an undiagnosed heart condition, Kate had fretted over medical anomalies.

She 'worried' the wooden tips of paint brushes with her teeth as a way to calm her nerves. And now she'd added Brigid to her worry list. If not for Maggie, Kate knew that she would end up going to bed way too early and then she would be awake in the middle of the night, worrying about her regrets.

The thought of worrying about Angus now that it was all over brought on new hunger pangs and she was grateful that she had a quick and easy fix for that. She sat down to remove her boots, and the sound from the small chair wasn't actually a groan. But it did intimate that the last thing she needed at this particular moment was to be carrying the extra weight of an unexpected single life.

And as she walked through the kitchen and into the solace of her white bedroom to change her clothes, her eyes found the open book and the highlighted words. They seemed to wink, as if she'd been missed, but that could have been from the tricky three-way light fixture that was now only operating on two planes.

She remembered all those earlier texts and tossed her phone onto the downy comforter. It bounced and Ross's forgotten business card followed. Had she left it to savor as she'd done with those moments in the various galleries, she wondered as she tried to quickly dry her hair.

Shedding her damp blouse, she looked around for something more comfortable to change into. "I can't let you keep doing this," Kate shouted as she looked at the idle phone, cradled and comfy in its man-made cocoon, and for the moment, perfectly quiet.

She picked up Ross's card and sat down on yet another ancient chair: white stock, black lettering, connected to Café G (a long initial in a small cursive style and bolder than the other letters), as he'd said. The letter looked like an inverted musical note hanging by the bars of a song.

It was an impressive card, until everything became all about removing the leggings that clung like a second skin. She leaned over, and the card, now laying on the floor beside her chair, seemed to beg for more attention as if it was aware that she'd missed the dark spot at the bottom righthand corner. Almost like a splotch of ink, but which turned out to be a stylized guitar. Something warm oozed through her insides. A sensual feeling that had to have come from the idea that besides his connection to the café, he was also a musician.

The phone rang. *Maybe Maggie cancelling?* Kate bent down and grabbed the ends of the leggings and ripped them off instead of letting the call go to voicemail. Then, she looked at the caller ID. "Shit!"

"What!" She snapped.

"Hello to you too," Angus replied.

"Texting wasn't enough?"

"I didn't think another text was appropriate; it's been a tough day, you know, and I just wanted to reach out."

"Yes, it's the same day as last year; how could I forget?"

"Please don't use that tone."

"What tone would you prefer?"

"I'm hurting too, Kate...really. I know I made a horrible mistake, but I'm truly sorry. Can't you try to let me back into your life?"

"Why would I do that?"

"Because down deep I know you still love me."

"Cocky bastard."

"Wait...don't hang up. I'm going to be in Portland next week, and I want—would like—to talk in person. I'll text you the day and time and the hotel...please consider it."

"YOU want ME to go to Portland to make you feel better...what's wrong with you." She swallowed hard and just as she was about to hang up, she shouted, "You're right, it's been a rotten day; don't call back!"

Why had she bothered to answer? She surmised all that he ever wanted was some sort of blessing that would give him permission to move on—the hell with the way her life might be crumbling apart.

Why hadn't she changed her number as Maggie had suggested. Or at least block his calls, which would have taken her out of his game-playing. No. She hadn't done either. And now she began to cry like she hadn't since the day she scribbled her signature on the courthouse papers.

When she was fully spent, she searched for one of the ribbons that she used to tie her hair, which was now shrieking at her in the mirror. And then, she threw on her mismatched yoga pieces, leftovers from classes she no longer took, but also large enough to hide a multitude of culinary sins. Contrary to popular belief about stress and food, she was suddenly ravenous!

She thought of the brief words she'd had with Angus, and like a child being forced into a time out, her slippers scuffed the wood flooring as she went back to the kitchen for something more palatable to digest. A mellow red wine was out on the counter alongside a stemless wine glass. The kind that nestled warmly into the palm of her hand.

It was all about stifling her anger, she thought as she yanked at the door on the fridge. But as she reached inside for the meatloaf, she pictured herself throttling Angus and the fridge made an odd noise as if it understood her intentions. And just then, she realized the meatloaf was sweating underneath the plastic wrap.

Ugh! She sniffed the meat. *Phew!* She looked heavenward and gave thanks that her mother's recipe hadn't gone to ruin and slid the plate into the microwave.

Her mind had carefully tended the picture of her parents at their table: first a blessing followed by the sign of the cross. And then. *Whatever came next?* Kate wondered. Her brain was on overload after all: the hours, the memories, the aromas and images of home. It was fast becoming one of the longest days of her life.

But the aroma of the loaf reminded her she needed to pull down her mother's round platter. It was part of a set of yellow and green plates that had once been part of the Hull Island set from her maternal grandparents. Everything else from her mother's own hope chest, was still in storage in a rental locker outside of Brunswick.

Kate sat down to admire the kitchen and wait for the meatloaf to become piping hot. The windows were completely dark now and might have seemed ominous if not for the bright yellow interior. And then, the entire room began to fill with the aroma of a mother's love on a plate. It was a perfect antidote to what had happened that day: her self-image; Angus and his constant interruptions; an intriguing business card and what it might mean if she saw the man again. She might as well add guilt over buying yet another book, she thought as she chalked it up on her mental scoreboard. Then, because she hated loose ends, she took out a pen and an always trusty yellow pad and began to work on a new list: Save/Donate.

It wasn't long before the coziness of the room and the wine mellowed her, made her whole body feel like it was melting from the inside out. She was *home* and that was a feeling she hadn't dared hope for after the past few years.

Brigid had remained on her mind as well, and how much it would mean to know the truths about *Summer Dreams*. Not to mention how often she'd strung her own metaphorical laundry throughout the Gardner all day.

Again, she found that she was losing her focus and she began to set those thoughts of Brigid aside, at least until she had all the titles down on paper.

Chapter 21

1936

August

Dear Diary,
I'm embarrassed to say that I would have done just about anything if I thought I would get away with it. In the past month, Jake has practically swallowed me whole with those deep brown eyes. His lips are sensuous, not hard-lined like my husband's, but then there's no comparing the two.

In the days during our 'sessions', Helen kept her word and took care of Tommy. I could only pray that during the times that she sat for Jake, that he wasn't looking at her in the same way, and I was too scared to ask.

We're supposed to meet again tomorrow, just Jake and me, and this time I'll take him up to the attic. This, whatever this is, could be my ruination. How will I ever be able to sneak him in or out even without anyone knowing.

September

Dear Diary,
I've waited to gather my thoughts, and yet I'm no clearer now. Except I do know that I have fallen in love for the first time in my life. Really in love, not what I thought I felt for Tim, who is the most

decent of all men, but a sensation that runs throughout my entire body and bends me into spasms of exquisite ecstasy. I could be standing at the sink and can be overtaken by this sensation faster than I can recover. What will I do now? James is due home in six days and Tommy is bound to mention all the time he's spent with auntie Helen.

Chapter 22

2018

Kate's head jerked to attention just as the pen hit the kitchen floor. She'd been dreaming—piles of books with torn pages and all of them being flung at Angus—and hadn't even heard the ding of the microwave. Knowing there wasn't much time left before Maggie would arrive, Kate practically inhaled the meatloaf and missed the finite notes of seasonings that her mother had used with such finesse. A lobster dinner was so routine, that a meatloaf became a feast for kings. Oh, how she missed the way her father would walk through the door wearing a smile and carrying a batch of weeds that melted Mary's heart. She'd cuff him affectionately on the shoulder and he'd scoop her up with his free arm and kiss her as if no one was watching.

And now her own exhaustion had unintentionally caused her to miss the opportunity to properly savor the one meal that she and her mother would make together when she was still a kid.

A resounding clang—the angry old knocker attacking the front door. Maggie had already dropped a big hint that the back door was in a 'creepy' spot, but Kate knew that it was because Maggie just loved that noisy piece of local history. It seemed it was the only thing that the landlord hadn't stripped away from the outside. "Back here, Maggie," Kate shouted. "And don't trip over the books!"

"I saw something like this on a TV show, but don't let that bother you." Maggie yelled back. "In case you're wondering, I'm taking my shoes off; it's nasty out there."

"*Collecting is not hoarding!*" Kate defended as the front door was slammed by the wind. "There's order in the chaos."

Maggie followed Kate's voice and found her sitting cross-legged on the floor in tan yoga pants and a tatty green sweatshirt. Her hair had been semi-tamed into a topknot. There was a half-empty glass on a small wooden footstool and a pile of books in front of her—the so-called 'order'. "Far be it from me to complain; I'm a collector of teacups, tureens and antique samplers."

"Maybe you could put some on the floor next time I come over."

"Now there's a thought."

Kate dropped her pen onto the yellow pad. Even in an oversized denim jacket, and designer jeans with supposedly fashionable cutouts, Maggie looked stunning. And with her blonde hair done up in a ponytail, younger than ever. "Did you have a good day?"

"Sort of, but what's all that about?" Maggie said with a broad sweep of her arm toward the living room. "I didn't know you had such a stash."

"I made the decision to buy another book about indoor plants and that turned into a whole other story. And now I'm stuck doing this," Kate said as she tossed the yellow pad to Maggie.

"Mine never made it through the year, but I tried."

"Maybe it was the salt air."

"Hmmm, maybe, or maybe it's just that I don't have your green thumb," Maggie said as she picked up a lacy maidenhair fern from the console.

"I almost wish I didn't, Kate said. "And that plant is not as difficult as you think it is, but I needed to finish organizing these books or I'll be overrun, and you'll have to come dig me out. Look at this giant book on landscaping…who needs this sucker?"

"A landscaper with huge muscles dressed in coveralls and a plaid shirt?"

"Not funny—that book led to cooking with edible flowers stacked alongside artists who painted flowers, which led to Giverney …in case you ever need to set a table—a la Monet."

"That's the book I stubbed my toe on, and yes, I'll take that one when I leave…big fan."

"Me too."

"Anything on how to roast and idiot, or say, the art of dealing with love in the wrong century?"

"How about, how to find a man without the internet?" Kate said.

"Ooh, a tad cranky, are we?"

"Sorry, didn't mean to sound so bitchy."

"Not to worry; you look tired."

"But I shouldn't take that out on you," Kate said.

"This can't all be about organizing your books."

"How to explain? "Kate said. "It has been an eye-opener of a day."

Maggie tilted her head, "Sorry?"

"It's complicated and as it turns out, I have three separate issues to deal with and they are somehow all lumped together," Kate said. "And I sure could have used your company."

"I thought I was doing you a favor."

"I know, but I still missed your support; I realized how much I missed those days with Angus that were really good."

"Do you mean to tell me you're actually considering taking him back!"

"Not! But he called again, and he's so much a part of my love for the Gardner," said Kate as she raised her hands in the air and pointed to the brochure that she'd brought home. "Then, there's Rembrandt; did I ever tell you that I talk to him?"

"Does he talk back?"

"Don't be obtuse; I confide in him, that's all."

"Okay, then what?"

"Then nothing, except when I say it to you, it helps to put things in perspective. And speaking of, did you know size zero jeans were the real deal and not just an urban myth?"

"According to my measuring tape, I think those days are gone forever," Maggie said.

"Mine too, but that's not the point. I used to love bumping into complete strangers, sharing, getting a feel for what was happening in the art world. And today, I had trouble getting out of my own way," Kate said. "But then maybe that's just an excuse because Angus has left the building.

"On top of that, I almost collided with an Angus look-alike as I was about to leave said building," Kate said.

"Now I'm all ears."

"I thought of you; the guy was really good looking?"

"What about thinking about yourself now that you're back on the market."

"Am I; it doesn't feel that way," Kate said, handing over the business card.

"Ooh, how sophisticated, Ross Anderson, and what do you do?" Maggie cooed as she held the card aloft.

"He's an events manager, see on the bottom."

"Not without my cheaters," Maggie said. "But did you at least bat those eyelashes of yours or encourage a meet-up?"

"Are we talking about dating or becoming a government informant?" Kate said.

"Now who's being obtuse; you could do with a little refresher course on the art of picking up men."

"I've never picked them up; just happened to be in the right place at the right time…hence my relationship with Angus," Kate said as she went into the kitchen to pour Maggie a glass of wine. "And today, I realized Angus is not really letting go and I don't know how to handle it."

"I told you to block his number or suffer the consequences," Maggie called after her.

"I know and I will; it's a process."

"Look on the bright side, for all his actions, at least he's not dead like my poor Edward," Maggie said as she took a sip. "Wow, a precocious red, just the type I like. What'd I do to merit this?"

"Good, right? And from what you've told me, Angus couldn't hold a candle to your Edward," said Kate as she refilled her own glass.

"So, what are we celebrating?"

"Honestly, I'm not sure, but you were right about my needing to go back to the Gardner, so we could toast to that if nothing else"

"Cheers, then, and I'm not always right, but the handwriting was right there in front of you."

"I know, and thank you," Kate said. "So how was your afternoon date?"

"Not really my type after all," Maggie said before taking another sip. "He's into pumping iron, unmemorable green drinks, and clean food—whatever that is…I mean, who eats dirty food."

"You, of all people, already know that it means no additives or chemicals, just lots of fresh stuff."

"Well, the way he talked, it sounded awful, and besides, he's not the brightest bulb even though he does possess a very healthy glow, like frosting." Maggie hung her head in mock shame. "That really was terrible."

"I've heard worse, but seriously, how do you keep doing this? I am obviously struggling with one divorce while you're out looking for a third Mr. Right."

"Can't help myself...I love being in love. Everything about it is appealing...oh, God, see what I mean," Maggie said. "I think that's how I survived losing Edward."

Kate tilted her head sideways and said, "By singing?"

"By remembering music like that, and the feelings that come over me afterward."

"But those songs, and your vocal range, who are you?"

"Obviously a lost woman," Maggie said.

"So, what about the young stud you had your eye on before Mr. Green?"

"Gorgeous guy...smart, artistic, and so not into me," Maggie said.

"Sorry."

"Anyway, if I wanted what I had, they'd have to bring my Edward back to life."

"I can't begin to imagine what it was like for you watching him after the accident, just waiting day after day in that hospital room with no hope in sight," Kate said. "But at least you know what it feels like to truly love and be loved back and that's not something everyone experiences."

"So why are you lamenting yours, then?"

"Just trying to convince myself it would have been easier if he hadn't left me for that blonde eye candy at the *Globe*—and how did I get to become such an afterthought?"

"You would have been happier if he'd cheated with some bling-wearing art collector from Back Bay?"

"No, but…"

"No buts about it; we're sad, sad women about to disappear if we don't do something and soon."

"But there's something else, and this may take a topping off before I'll be able to tell you."

"Okay, but you know you can tell me anything, right?"

"Yes, but I'd buried this for so long, and then today, it all came flooding back," Kate said as she refilled their glasses.

"I'm listening, and I will not judge, I promise you."

"I had an abortion," Kate blurted. "And before you say anything, I'm not sorry I did, but I am furious at myself for not telling Angus at the time."

"May I ask why?"

"I like to think that it was because I was so young and inexperienced, but I now think it was because I was too embarrassed to tell him that I'd never actually wanted kids," Kate said, the words running out of her before she could change her mind. "And when I got pregnant, I was afraid he'd want me to give up my dreams and be a stay-at-home mom.

"Then today I saw these little kids and…"

"And you wish you'd had a second chance?"

"No, that's just it…I wasn't at all like my mom, not even a smidgeon of motherhood floated through my Irish veins. Nothing of the domestic except cooking and without someone to cook for, I'm even losing that desire.

"Or I could say it was because I was still such a kid myself and let myself off the hook, but really, I just buried it all, and now you'll think I'm a horrible person. I know my family would have."

"On the contrary," Maggie said. "Edward and I always talked about a large family but never really acted on those conversations.

"And when he died, those dreams died with him, and unless I'm mistaken, I'm beyond my childbearing years.

"And can you imagine what my life would be like if I'd had kids with that *asshat* I married next?"

"Asshat?"

"Edward's favorite saying, stolen from a murder mystery novel and turned into his very own catchphrase."

"You really don't think I'm a horrible person for not telling Angus?"

"In hindsight, no, because he might have cheated anyway, and a grown child would then have become your crutch, and think of how stunted he or she would have felt escorting you around and making your meals and cleaning up after you."

"Are we talking about my fictional child or the very handsome *youngster* you had your eye on?"

"How about we change that subject so that you can appreciate the life you've made for yourself."

"Thanks for not judging me; it's really all that deep-seated Catholic guilt that I walked right into when I spotted Boticelli's *Virgin and Child*. Not only do I feel extra-round like the women in his paintings, but on the ride home I thought of my mom and all the things that might have been had she lived. And, that nearly destroyed me."

"Good thing you have me then," Maggie said. "Can we eat, drink and be a little bit merrier and come up with a new game plan."

"Any suggestions?"

"Yes; don't change your mind about a date with my brother, or…"

Kate left Maggie mid-sentence, and said, "Hang on a sec."

"I thought we were talking about Paul?"

"In a minute, but first I need to show you something," Kate said coming back into the room. "This is the other thing I needed to share with you, but I had to grab the photo first."

Maggie pulled the cheaters from her jacket pocket and bending over the photo, said, "Wow, what a likeness!"

Brigid appeared like a goddess set against the backdrop of an unrelenting sky that just happened to match a blue drape in some miscellaneous fabric that had turned her from a housewife into a siren. Kate offered a similar smile and said, "This is what I'm supposed to be."

"A model?"

"No, just naturally photogenic."

"You don't even know how lovely you are; Paul will notice."

"Thanks, but it isn't so much about being noticed as it is about getting back the woman I was before I got sucked into the tragedy known as Angus's love triangle."

"A bit Shakespearian don't you think?"

"That's exactly what I mean; before we split, Angus called me a shrew!"

"Now that's something you've never mentioned."

"Who'd want to?"

"So, who's this," Maggie asked as she pointed to the other woman in the photo.

"I won't know until I talk with my dad again, and I'm thinking I'll still have to rummage through my storage unit," Kate said. "When I moved back, I just tossed everything in there, including my mother's personal things."

"There are mixed messages all over this," Maggie said extending her arm. "All that flowy material, soft skin, cold gray stone trimmed in lacey lichen. And those shadowed tree trunks with watchful eyes."

"Those are woodpecker holes you nit."

"Still, it's sending a message," Maggie said. "And the artist?"

"It's way down in the right corner...Giacomo Canelli, but again, not a known artist, at least not where I've checked."

"I've never heard of him either," Maggie said.

"But now I'm obsessed with finding him."

"You have to bring this photo with you when you meet Paul," Maggie said.

"Why?"

"Because he knows a lot about art, that's why, and besides he'll see the resemblance and find you enchanting."

"Enchanting! God, Maggie, what's gotten into you?"

"Well, just look at her—look at the way your gran is looking at him...like they'd already had sex on the lawn," Maggie said. "Sorry, my mind again."

"You really have a case."

"Of what I'm not sure. Then again, it could be my unruly hormones. Edward always said I was a hot ticket," Maggie said. "But back to Brigid; where did they meet?"

"It had to have been here on Hull Island, and you're blushing."

"Let's concentrate on my favorite thing in this entire painting...those shadows," Maggie said.

Kate eyeballed the elongated tree in the foreground, the alchemy created by the cobalt and Prussian blues that she'd worked out, but they'd been mixed with a rose color she couldn't identify. "I have scoured my brain for how this formula came to be, but so far nothing."

"Somehow, I always forget that little factoid about you; why don't you paint anymore?"

"Okay, third surprise—I think I'd like to start up again," Kate said. "Don't hold me to it, but I'm considering it, just for fun."

"And for profit I hope?"

"We'll see, but for now, could we talk about you for a while?"

"Sure, but that includes Paul too; I know you guys would hit it off."

"I wish I was so sure," Kate said. But I also wish I'd said I had plans when Angus called; maybe he'd leave me alone."

"What?"

"He wanted us to meet next week."

"And you would have *used* Paul as your go-to excuse?"

"I hadn't thought of it that way."

"I'm just teasing, but I hope with all my heart that you and my brother really click," Maggie said.

"And if it all goes well, you and I might have some awkward conversations later, won't we. You know, the ones that you like to have after you've been to bed with a new guy."

"Ohmygod, I never thought of that."

"I have," Kate said. "But maybe it's the waning Gibbous moon."

"Maybe it's just that neither of us have had sex in longer than we'd care to remember," Maggie said. "Whoops, that was a bit rude."

"You're not, and honestly, I don't know if I remember how that works anymore."

"I'm not going to throw in the bicycle analogy, but trust me, it'll come back to you very quickly, and I'm going to set a date for dinner at my place."

"Does he really know a lot about paintings?"

"Great segue," Maggie said.

Picking up the photo, Kate said, "Since tonight's turned into a tell-all, *Summer Dreams* was the reason I happened to run into you at the Farnsworth in the first place."

"I thought it was because you were another huge fan of Andrew Wyeth's work".

"I am, but I'd been at the gift shop browsing long before I swung by the Wyeth Center where I spotted you, and of course, the rest is history."

"Did I ever tell you that Edward gave me a small original as a wedding present. We used to go as far as Chads Ford, Pennsylvania, for his exhibits."

"I'm glad we met, whatever the reason," Kate said. "And I wish I could find out the truth about what happened to Brigid."

"You know me and research, maybe I can help."

"Yes, I know you spend enough time at the library to have a wing named after you," Kate said. "But research won't tell you about all the goings on behind frilly gingham curtains, which I once overheard my parents talking about when they didn't know I was out on the back stoop."

"You mean like swingers?" Maggie said.

"What would you know about *that* Miss Maggie?"

"Just what I've been told, Miss Kate—but there was one nutjob I went out with who invited me to join a group over in Topsham."

"You're kidding!"

"Naturally, I didn't go," Maggie said. And truthfully, I miss Edward more than I can say. On top of that, I regret my second marriage, and now I can't seem to get it right."

"Is that why you've been going on about finding a lover instead of a husband this time around?"

"Yes, and I think that would be simply splendid, and a lot less time consuming."

"Not sure I could go that route."

"It's never too late."

"Maybe, but if I did find love again, I think I'd like it to be with someone who could watch old movies or go to a play and not feel the need to crit every little detail," Kate said. "Maybe even someone who would rub my back after a big day at the easel, presuming I'm going to paint again."

"Personally, I'd like to find someone who could dance me to the end of love."

"Whoa".

"Right, but it's true; Edward and I danced all over the house, wherever there was a bare floor, which means lots of different rooms—what can I say."

"Not much after that," Kate said as she topped off their glasses.

"Your face looks thinner; have you lost some weight."

"Hardly," Kate said as she moved toward the refrigerator. "But let me cut up some carrot sticks to go with our wine and cheese."

"Don't you dare!" Maggie said. "But first things first—Paul is fifty-four, around five eleven, same brown eyes, but not my sparkling personality."

"Well, I can't give you someone to spice up your life, but I've found something at the Gardner apropos of your sparkling personality," Kate said. "But you have to wait for your birthday to see."

"You mean you've found me my perfect match?"

"Don't be snide," Kate said although she had initially thought about introducing her to Ross.

"It's all Cohen's fault."

"Leonard Cohen?" Kate said.

"The one and only," Maggie said. "After Edward, he's been the one to cheer me on, reminding me what it feels like to really love someone with all my heart."

"In that case, we better fasten our seatbelts," said Kate raising a glass.

"To all the dances to come," replied Maggie as she reached for the bottle of wine.

Chapter 23

1936

September

Dear Diary,
 I don't know how long I can get away with sending Tommy off to Helen's; his questions are growing bolder by the minute. He thought it was odd that I had on my good fall dress the other day; he knows I only have two and that I wear them for special occasions. He also said that I smelled funny, which was kinda sweet because I never wear perfume, but that day I'd used some rosewater that had been a gift from my mother. My little boy is too wise for his age, but while he'd been with Helen, my head was being filled with rants about Hopper and Kent and God knows who, which was Jake trying to enlighten me about the artists he reveres. He keeps talking about Monhegan and a colony of artists who'd made their name out on that stark island, not that I understood why anyone would want to go through such hardship just to create a painting.
 And then, each time Jake leaves, my mind roams out to the Cathedral Wood that he talked about, leaving me to wonder what it would be like to have a small hideaway built for a clutter-free life. A tiny nook for my child and a place to feed on love. Who am I becoming and what will happen if I don't stop now.
 Helen finally knows what's been going on and she says she understands, though she still wishes it were her. In a way, I do too; she's free to feel the love I want, free as the birds to have an affair of the heart and of the body. I am bound by the laws of God and the will of James Flannagan and I'm afraid.

Chapter 24

2018

A wee pickaxe disguised as a clock bashed against Kate's brain. In contrast, a quiet light had ascended on her bedroom. A crow sheltered in a branch offered his own opinion of the morning. And displayed the same impatience that he had ever since she'd moved in and begun feeding him.

She rose from her misery with unabashed reluctance, but coffee was imperative. And without a doubt, the body trying to put one foot in front of the other, wasn't really hers, but that of a woman whose bones had already compressed, whose hair had grayed, and whose teeth had to be rinsed instead of brushed. What had she been thinking with all that wine!

As the tendrils of coffee floated from her ancient espresso maker, the crow's repetitive cry seemed to scream 'lightweight' instead of 'feed me'. She certainly was lightheaded, and the aroma of a fresh brew seemed to add rather than subtract from her condition. But as she padded over to the little powder room, she was distracted from her churning stomach by how little her landlord had done with what could have been made into a tiny showstopper. For some reason, a powder room hadn't seemed cut out for his manly skills, but since there were so many pluses it hadn't mattered at the time. But now that she'd been here a while and fallen in love with the place, she constantly picked apart what had once been an iddy-biddy slant-roofed closet. The framing was still exposed, and he'd dropped a miniature sink into a scavenged nightstand. An extra-long chain hung from the ceiling mount, which caused her to flail her arms about in order to keep it away from her face. There would be no flailing this morning either, not in her present state. She'd been given one of those candles that came in a glass jar with a lid and now she uncapped it in hopes that the outdoorsy fragrance would clear her head. And before she could light it, she decided she didn't need to be in here; she needed something sugary like the jelly she'd bought at the farmer's market that paired nicely with a large slab of bread—purchased before she'd made that pact with herself and now needed to be defrosted. Then, she realized the date, and vowed to start her grand plan on April Fool's Day just in case she couldn't go through with it.

The more she thought about the previous night, the more she realized that it had been much more than simply getting things off her chest. It had turned into a scrubbing clean of all misdeeds, and that had taken a lot of confidence in her friendship with Maggie. If only it hadn't taken so much alcohol, she thought, as she took her cup back into her bedroom. And now, it still comes down to what to wear to meet Paul. Maggie had been curious about the way Kate had dressed for her dates with Angus, and all she could say was that during those days, clothes came off more often than not. And now, she couldn't possibly imagine being that comfortable with someone ever again. The only thing she could be sure of as she nestled back against the down pillows, was that she wouldn't be wearing black.

Kate was startled from sleep and a lengthy lucid dream obviously predicated on last night's conversation. The memory of a diary. She'd recalled that her mother, during one of her diatribes about the church, had gone to the attic, supposedly to clean. When in fact, it was the one place that Mary could air out her differences in private.

Last night had brought back subconscious memories, things said during the week she'd moved her father into the assisted living facility in Brunswick. Something about having to repair a hole under the eaves in the attic. He'd rambled on about her mother's sewing boxes and Kate had assumed he meant for her to store them away for safekeeping. And now everything was stored away in a locked unit. And if she wanted to sort them, she first had to find the key. She'd been clumsy about stuff like that when she moved back to Maine. Had paid far more attention to her bruised ego than to her father's ramblings. But now it was dizzying to think she might actually have something as precious as Brigid's diary somewhere among her personal possessions.

The crow suddenly screeched, one of those long, drawn-out sounds that made her want to throttle him. She rolled over and thought of Paul and wondered how he felt about the sunrise or what he might be thinking about meeting her.

And then she thought of Maggie again, and she knew that meeting Paul would be okay. And fun. And that's not something she'd had in a very long time.

Six-thirty and Kate was right on time. Not that Maggie hadn't already double-checked that she would be as if Kate would do a runner instead. Someone had already scraped at the dark brown paint that was original to the cottage, someone who may have been thinking of painting it a far less drab shade. But obviously Maggie had given up, Kate thought as she wrapped the knuckles of her free hand against the door. She waited a minute and knocked again, and when she heard Maggie's voice on the other side, she walked into a plain, but proper sized mudroom just as Maggie was pocketing her cell phone.

"Am I early?" Kate said.

"Sorry about that," said Maggie. "You're here and that's all that matters."

"Everything okay?"

"Just Paul, saying he was close by, not to worry."

"Sounds like we're both having the jitters."

"Don't be silly; here let me take that from you…looks luscious."

"Chocolate pie on a tin plate, buried under whipped cream, foolproof," Kate said as she followed Maggie into the kitchen. "You really do collect tureens!"

"I forgot, you haven't been in here since I moved things around," Maggie said, "but I call the whole bunch spontaneous happiness."

An array of lidded-China bowls crowned a bank of light gray pine cupboards that were also original to the old cabin. The quirkiness of the tureens had been highlighted by the ecru walls. They automatically perked up the space where dust lurked and no one cared. "They are simply wonderful!" Kate said.

"I don't use them nearly enough, but at least I get them down for holidays. Getting out the ladder is a bother, and then that leads to cleaning I hadn't planned on, but some of them are quite valuable."

"So, when you teased me about all my books all over the floor, you were just teasing about leaving these out for me to trip over, right."

"And you won't let me forget that."

"Probably in about five or ten years," Kate said.

"You still brooding over Angus?"

"Not tonight, I promise."

"Good." Maggie held up a bottle of white with a fancy French label and said, "Let's have a glass of this while we wait."

"A bit of déjà vu here?" Kate said lifting up one of the delicate wine glasses to make it easier for Maggie to pour. "Did you happen to have any luck with Google?"

"My head, thanks to the hours spent in your very colorful and cozy cottage, which by the way helped solidify the way I also feel about our friendship, prevented me from doing very much," Maggie said. "I knew we would be good friends the moment we met, but trust is a whole other issue. And for you to trust me with all that, well what can I say, it's the best birthday gift a girl could ever want."

"You'll still get a gift on the date, but I did the right thing telling you," Kate said as she hugged Maggie tightly.

"You'll make me cry, kiddo, and that's not good for my eyeliner and besides we don't want Paul asking lots of questions.

"But back to Canelli, it looks like he spent time in Paris, and then, it was like he disappeared off the face of the earth," Maggie said.

"It was eye-opening for me too, and now all I have to do is find a key to the storage unit so I can look for Brigid's diary."

"You didn't say anything about *that* last night, did you?"

"I only remembered it this morning."

"Hold that thought; I see headlights."

Kate heard a car door slam. And the mud room door open. Then laughter, and Paul's voice—confident and warm. Intriguing. Nothing to be nervous about, except wishing she had worn a longer sweater over her tight-fitting jeans. She had begun to lose a little weight, but still.

"I'm glad you've started without me," Paul said as he walked over with an outstretched hand. "It's nice to finally put a face to the name."

"You, too." Kate felt the warmth of his palm with its hint of moisture...was he nervous too. He placed a bottle of domestic Chardonnay on the counter and then poured himself a glass from the already opened bottle. She studied his profile—his coloring, mannerisms, the solidness of an average build, a very small scar on his chin. Unintentional comparisons to the man she'd just professed she hadn't been thinking about.

"Behind," Maggie said.

Kate scooched over toward Paul and wondered if Maggie's little move to open the oven door was intentional. "Smells fabulous!"

"Is that your moussaka, sis?"

"I'm not going to say you shouldn't have gone to so much trouble, because I love anything with lamb," Kate said.

Maggie grinned at them, saying, "See you already have a lot in common."

"Ignore her, Kate. She is just trying to get under my skin."

"I know the feeling; is there a cure for her condition?"

"They don't allow brothers to muzzle their sisters in America these days."

"As if they ever did," Maggie said. "But you could fill the water glasses."

"Want me to cut the bread too?"

"Yes, please."

Teasing quickly took a back seat to Maggie's wonderful culinary effort, the list of items used to make such a profound work of art in one dish. She had overlapped the eggplant slices to envelope the thick creamy bechamel and encase the lamb and the aroma filled the room. Kate found herself letting go as she listened to brother and sister slinging their verbal arrows that reeked of love and friendship and kindness. "This casserole smells amazing!"

Paul winked at her. It seemed an affirmation to both her comment and her presence. She was now part of their banter, their teamwork even if she was only there to observe the way he skillfully cut up an ordinary French baguette. Or the manner in which he grabbed the plates that had been warming on top of the stove, balancing them against his sleeved arm to avoid burning himself even though she attempted to help. He shook his head and smiled just as Maggie added a double helping to the plate he was holding for Kate.

The siblings moved in concert and she noticed that Paul kept one eye on her as well. It was an interesting dynamic because neither her father or Angus ever set foot in the kitchen. And without losing a beat, Paul said, "Maggie tells me you're a Rembrandt afficionado."

Kate paused until he'd put all the plates down on the table, and he and Maggie had taken their seats before she said, "Let's just say I like to keep an eye on him from time to time."

"What an interesting concept," Paul said. "Like you can protect him…and if so, from what?"

"Sounds a lot sillier when put like that, but I guess it's partly because he—his painting—barely escaped being stolen from the Gardner, and …" Kate's cheeks spontaneously flushed.

"And?"

Paul wasn't used to her; something like this was bound to fall on deaf ears, and she wasn't up for any type of argument. Or a puffed-up opinion of any kind, which she supposed she expected after so many years with Angus. She waited until Maggie turned her attention to her plate and then shrugging her shoulders, Kate said, "It's such a long story, and right now I'd really like to hear more about you."

"Besides what Mags has already told you, and I know she has, I'm an insurance broker."

"I'm not sure I know what that is."

"Let's say you're older and you need health insurance and there's all this complicated stuff to sift through. That's when you call me. I come to your home and we run through your medical needs and what you think you can manage, and I search the various companies and come up with the perfect plan!"

"My brother, the genius," Maggie said.

"No, just diligent, and I get a lot of pleasure from seeing those same clients every fall when open enrollment comes around."

Kate watched closely as Paul's cheeks colored. "You have a passion for what you do; that's admirable."

"And you seem to have a passion for art."

"She studied in Boston," Maggie said.

How could she possibly recreate the pace of her life the way that she had reconstructed it at the Gardner just days before. Instead, she smiled and said, "Just for a while; then life happened as it does with everyone and I moved on from being a student to just being a follower. And that's kind of why I remained such a fan of the Great Masters. But really, the rest is way too boring for tonight."

"Then, maybe we can have a proper date…unchaperoned," Paul said.

"Yay!"

"Maggie!" Kate said.

"Sorry."

"No, she's not, but you'll get used to it, and besides in our family she was known as a wannabe Blanche Devereaux, you know, from the *Golden Girls*."

"You're kidding!"

"Let's have some of that dessert before..."

"Before what, Maggie? You toss me out on the street and lock the door like you used to?" Paul said biting back his laughter.

"We were kids."

"Doesn't matter; it left me scarred for life!"

Now Kate saw the real bond, not just the repartee used for guests, and she sensed a new form of envy. And even if she had never wanted kids, she just realized how wonderful it would have been to be able to share secrets with a sibling of her own. An older brother like Paul might have kept her from making some of the mistakes she had with Angus. But of course, many things looked better in hindsight. Thinking of her mother's commentary on behavior, Kate smiled and said, "Considering the brutality of your childhood, you both seemed to have held up rather well."

"It's all a façade," Paul said. "You only see her good side; she can be brutal."

"Give me a break," Maggie said as she pulled his empty plate off the table.

"Hey, I might want seconds!"

"Kate made dessert."

"My cue; let me serve, please." Kate said with a smirk.

"Just a small piece for me," Maggie said.

"I'll have her share, Kate," Paul said. "And please don't think badly of us; we get like this when Maggie drinks."

"Me!" Maggie yelped.

"Picture this, guys; how about I cut equal pieces and you just eat what you want," Kate said.

"I like your style," Paul said. "By the way, sis told me a little about the situation with your grandmother's painting. Have you considered there might be a love-child out there?"

Suddenly, the room's aura changed. "Actually, no."

"That might be a good topic over a drink and dinner—without my sister."

"We could make her suffer." Kate realized she'd moved right into their dynamic and suddenly there was nothing to fear. She had built up a wall for no reason and yet...

"I'm right here guys," Maggie said.

"Great idea," Paul said as he scooped a large piece of pie into his mouth. "And how about teaching Maggie about pie making, Kate."

Maggie slapped him a little harder than expected, but she winked at Kate. "Foil is in the top right-hand drawer; maybe you'd like to wrap up the rest for Paul."

"I guess that's my cue to leave," Paul said as he took the foil away from Kate and wrapped the remainder of the pie. "Pay her no mind, Kate, I have an early morning call and I will be in touch."

"Let me walk you out, brother dear."

Kate's head was about to burst from trying to keep up, but there was an unexpected flutter in her chest.

Paul had looked at her with the intensity of a man on a mission. "This is crazy," she whispered as she began to clear the rest of the dishes.

The outer door banged and Maggie walked into the kitchen, "I'll take care of those later."

"I'll just wrap the rest of the moussaka and then I'll be off."

"He likes you."

"He's very nice, but let's not get ahead of ourselves, okay?"

"I know my brother."

"Not tonight, please."

"We'll talk," Maggie said.

"I'll call you tomorrow, and again, thank you for absolutely everything, and you're a great cook."

"You're most welcome, drive safe."

Paul had indeed been a surprise, although all things considered, Kate should have expected him to be so at ease, so like Maggie. But it was more; he cared about people, which was far more important than his looks. Yet, dating had obviously changed since she and Angus met, and even they had made up their own rules as they went along. Flashes of their early days sped through her brain as she rounded the turn just in time to see a curl of water crash over one of the roadside boulders.

She'd left the window down to clear her head and to allow for the sound that was predictable. One that she loved dearly, just as she loved the entirety of the Maine coast. And it had only taken a divorce and associated heartbreak to bring her back home to the sea that grew enormous under the moon. The stars that could never be found above a cityscape. The things that had mattered and belonged to childhood and the Flannagan house. And especially to the beating heart of an island where she and Angus might have grown old.

Kate stepped inside her house and immediately noticed that other beating heart: the pulsating red associated with her new answering machine.

Paul or Maggie? Play it or save till morning? Her index finger hovered over the button for a few seconds before giving in. The tone of Paul's voice cut through the silence of the room; his tone hinting at what his interest in her might be, other than the missing painting.

But she'd finally come to understand how easy it would be to fall in step with someone else's intentions. She simply wasn't up for more bantering with a charming bachelor, not tonight. Instead, she walked through to her bedroom and the lovely vignette, the scene of a single woman intent on a peaceful coexistence with her surroundings. And of course, books, plenty of books. Somewhere among them was the solution to the mystery that she'd read again and again and always with the hope of a different outcome.

A cookbook she hadn't opened in years, and a police procedural she hadn't opened at all, as if she already knew where the famous detective would find his culprit.

Which book would lull her into dreamland tonight? Certainly not the harbinger of bad news in the dramatic tale about a woman who had survived cancer, twice or even the 'three time's a charm' wedding of a divorcee that Maggie had loaned her.

Kate looked around the room, her eyes searching to see if she'd missed a book among the clutter, one that she'd had to have only a week ago. And just like that, it was as if she'd been cuffed upside the head—how could she even think of sharing all of this with *any* man!

But you never expected to meet a guy like Paul, right?

Chapter 25

1936

October

Dear Diary,

Jake went out to Monhegan for two whole weeks and has returned with new paintings and a sunburned face. The holidays are right around the corner, and now I have to worry each and every day about what's going to happen to me when James returns from his latest trip. Jake wants to go back to Monhegan with the other artists, supposedly to scout around for a place of his own, but says he'll only be gone for a few days.

How is it possible that I've fallen so hard for this man: his ability to poke fun of himself, his intense passion for his work, and even the images he paints with words about a place I've never seen.

His intensity heats the air in our love nest, even on the coldest days. The attic has become a world unto itself and when he's here, I become a beguiling creature while he creates wonderful sketches of me.

I have such a very bad case that even Helen is sympathetic, but of course she's been in this situation before. She knows how distressing love can be. She also knows that Jake accomplished very little while she'd been sitting for him, only a few rather pretty drawings, although it did highlight all her best features. But it certainly lacked the impact with which he has drawn me. He says he is going to paint the two of us into the final painting, that it will balance the perspective and the provocativeness of the theme. I have no idea what that all means, but I want to see the finished product and I want Helen to be a part of this too. She has to be, or I'm afraid our friendship might not survive...especially after he leaves Hull Island for good.

It's already apparent how much she's changed because of my attachment to Jake. But I miss our sisterly bond. Sometimes the guilt chokes me when I look into her eyes and see what she sees.

Somehow, she still takes care of Tommy while I'm with Jake, and without complaint, but her bravado is false and more evident as time goes by.

I dreamt about Tim last night, which is unusual these days. He was with his pals Hap Nickerson and Bob Wiley and there was a car so they must have been off on one of their many escapades. And in this dream, Tim stood out and made me laugh and when I woke up, I remembered how he loved taking long rides through the countryside on Sunday afternoons. I thought those stolen kisses were the most exciting and wonderful thing in the world until Jake turned up and introduced me to tenderness and warmth and sexual gratification...love at a level I never knew existed. The guilt should be eating me alive, but that's the thing, I'm more alive than I've ever been. And while I know it's wrong to wish one's husband away at sea longer than he's in port, I pray that the man who has introduced me to the joys of lusty behavior, will never leave me alone again. For what do I really have without him? Who will I grow old with besides Tommy. And he is destined for the sea like all the other young boys on the island.

At least Jake has promised to finish my painting before going back to Monhegan, because he is determined to join with the best artists who make that pilgrimage. Then, he casually said, "come with me" and I almost said yes. But even if I went for a few days and left Tommy with my parents or with Helen, which would be like throwing salt on a wound, I couldn't chance it. That would give James the perfect reason to take my boy away from me, and I would die.

I'm already beginning to notice people whispering when they see me at the market or the post office; there will be hell to pay if that *gossip reaches James's ears. I use all my wits to ignore those women by acting snooty and forcing them to turn away. Not a very neighborly thing for me to be doing, but then, nothing I'm doing has anything to do with being a good neighbor.*

Fortunately for me, James had to stop at a port in New Jersey for some repair or other, and isn't due to return just yet. I'd rather his stopover was due to a love nest of his own, but that might be too much to wish for.

Chapter 26

2018

Kate opened her eyes expecting to find musicians in her bedroom; the dream had centered on flamenco guitars and the colors of the Spanish countryside. In this first light, her walls as if somehow picking up on that dream, looked like they'd been dusted in beige, what she would have considered a non-color. And yet, if she turned her head just so, the color might be considered pale maple sugar, the way it looked in candy form, not the pouring type. Dreaming had taken on a whole new type of intensity since her visit to the Cloister. And when she sat up, the walls had changed again, picking up on the sultry morning sky. How grand it would be to stay in bed and pretend the day away, but she stood instead, only to find that her toes rebelled against the cold floor. But her inner voice told her to ignore her slippers and walk barefoot across an imaginary sand beach where magically food would appear: one egg, a thin slice of whole grain bread, and coffee of course. But in real time, she put a pan of cold water on the stove and pulled out the toaster and then while she waited, she dialed Maggie's number, counting the rings until the machine kicked in. "You must be in the shower," Kate said. "Just me, wanting to say thanks again and well, what can I say about your brother. Except that he left me a message last night and it's too early to reply, and I'm confused but also flattered about his dinner invitation. Please call!"

It was obviously too soon to know how it would pay off, but she was finally motivated; no more pie or any bad carbs until she saw solid results. Now if she could just do the same with her wardrobe and find something that would put a lilt in her step without making her look like she was trying too hard. So many of her things were made well, which is why she'd been inclined to keep them all these years, but they were definitely out of style.

Within minutes, Kate's bed was covered in jackets, slacks and jeans as well as sweaters pulled from the now empty dresser drawers. Things that were in really good condition would be donated to the local thrift shop, and the rest, like her ratty jeans, would simply be tossed out. But there was one jacket, a dusty pink boucle with a hint of blue in the threads that happened to still be in vogue. It also picked up the color of her eyes, and it had shoulder pads that gave it a retro yet modern look. She would definitely have to keep it unbuttoned, but if she added a mock turtleneck in the right shade of blue, she could pull it off.

She tried it on and spun around, and just then her phone rang; she picked it up before it could go to voicemail. "Good morning sleepyhead, too much wine last night?"

"Don't be so sassy; I was in the shower as you suspected," Maggie said. "Have you called my brother yet?"

"Absolutely not…it's way too early and I haven't finished my coffee," Kate said reaching for the cup.

"He's an early riser and you should catch him *before* his day starts or you might end up playing phone tag."

"So?"

"So, nothing. Just take my advice, call the guy so he can breathe."

"Very dramatic."

"No, just practical; I saw how he looked at you."

"What are you up to today?"

"There you go changing the subject, but for your information, I'm going to be doing more research…but not on your Canelli."

"He's not mine; are you back on toxins again?"

"Yes, there's a study that was done on the Pease Tradeport water system three years ago that I need to review."

"How's your New Hampshire friend holding up?"

"Not well, but that would take hours of conversation and I don't want to hold up your day either," Maggie said. "I'll give you the full scoop next time I see you, but in the meantime…call Paul!"

"All right! And I promise I'll let you know, after, okay?"

"Fine!"

"You can hang up now, I won't change my mind," Kate said.

"Hanging up now…have a great day."

The phone went dead before Kate could reply. And then it rang again.

"What now?"

"Sorry?"

"Oh god, I thought it was your sister."

"I know it's early, but I also didn't want to get on the road where I wouldn't have a chance to talk."

"I really was going to call; you just beat me to it."

"I've got to be in Brunswick tomorrow; any chance I can take you to dinner?

Kate took a deep breath, thought of her options and said, "I'd like that, what time?"

"How about I pick you up around six, if that's good."

"I planned on seeing my father tomorrow; why don't I just meet you."

"Do you like the Nobel Tavern?"

"I do…see you there at six?"

"Great; looking forward to it."

Kate hung up and turned to look at her reflection, and what looked to be an egg in the untamed nest on top of her head. There was no way she could get a last-minute appointment at the salon in Brunswick. Instead, she grabbed a cap and stepped into her spa-like shower—the unimaginable luxury designed by the man who would wear stripes and plaids together—her landlord, Buddy Knox. Letting the water cascade down her body, she ran through the requirements for her client, the very dapper Harry Morgan, who would be at her office at nine sharp.

When she stepped out, she burst out laughing. The facial masque she had intended to use this morning was still on the edge of the sink and now there was no time for pampering. Again, her eyes roamed around the luxurious room, only this time she decided it had to have been the idea of the peculiar woman who'd turned out to be the realtor Buddy had hired when he'd contemplated selling rather than renting.

Toweling off, Kate pondered the word peculiar, and the other client she would face today. Ethyl Smoot was the last appointment of the day and she was all about her cat Tilda. Kate's imperative was to remain kind but also state that Tilda could not be claimed as a dependent. No matter how many receipts Ethyl dragged in and plopped on Kate's desk. She would also have to listen to Ethyl's rants that the cat was as much of a dependent as her now divorced daughter, and who was the IRS anyway, to tell her the cat's necessities weren't a plausible deduction.

Kate always bookended those two clients because they both required a special skill set and because of the way she would expect someone to treat her father during his slow decline from reality.

Kate always felt this was her duty and also a privilege; she might not have asked to be an accountant and years ago would have preferred her name on a large poster in front of a notable gallery. But like Paul, she truly enjoyed helping people. And quite suddenly she realized that contained within her concerns, was the realization that she was looking forward to that dinner date after all.

She stepped out into the morning and stopped in her tracks as she identified wave clouds, a rare spring phenomenon, which had to be a good omen. As if they'd been curated to make her feel good about almost anything. Like the tan slacks she'd chosen to go with a tan turtleneck, a singular tone to slim her down and also looked smart with her leather jacket instead of the boucle. And a little bit of black never really hurt anyone, or at least not this particular black. The soft leather looked and felt expensive, even though she'd found it during a black Friday sale when she lived in Boston.

Harry was actually there when she arrived, as if he hoped to escort her inside, his flirtatious nature just waiting to show itself. Never mind that he was married to a fabulous and stylish woman who ran circles around him. Kate couldn't begin to understand the dynamics of other people's marriages, but she did her best during their hour-long session to make Harry feel understood. And then after he left, she combed through his records in the quiet of her cubicle, rehashing his concerns and though he really didn't need much help, she understood it was all about garnering attention and she was a good listener. His wife, Marjory, always sent a note at Christmas, thanking Kate for giving her the time to shop for family presents in peace. Marriage, Kate thought, the ultimate conundrum.

Ethyl had been a different sort today. Her complexion verified that she'd been recovering from a stomach bug since their last appointment. And instead of going on about Tilda, she complained about the fact that she'd been too infirm to keep her nail appointment and now felt hideous. *I caught the damn bug from my beau,* Ethyl had said. Kate had suspected that Ethyl had a man in her life; she'd been amping up the perfume and buying clothes that she'd never looked at before. And she always explained her color and style choices, like she and Ethyl were BFFs. But this afternoon, Ethyl had been thoroughly pissed, adding that she would no longer be keeping company with a man who in actuality was looking for a 'nurse with a purse'. Kate had stopped what she was doing and groaned. What a conversation! And now she kept rehashing it frame by frame as she drove to Thornton Oaks to see her father.

And then it hit her, hard—she no longer had anyone to grow old with. She didn't have a lot of income to look forward to, not like Ethyl. But that whole nurse/purse scenario made her laugh so hard that she had to pull over to the side of the road. There wasn't a man around who could get the best of old Ethyl, not by a long shot. But Kate could hardly wait to share that little nugget with Maggie, without impugning Ethyl's reputation of course. It was too bad that she couldn't have a laugh about it with her dad.

It had been enough to get him to believe his new residence suited him well without saying something negative about group living. And that's basically what it was…meals together, exercise and showtimes in the lounge. It was a wonderful fit for him and they'd spent plenty of time together flushing out the right one. In the end, Thornton Hall gave him all that he needed to cope without Mary. Even a cooking space that he used before he forgot where he put things. Kate had initially thought it was because of the unfamiliarity of the building itself, but now that he'd been diagnosed with early onset Alzheimer's, none of that mattered.

Kate wondered if Ethyl had ever looked at Thornton before deciding on the place in Topsham. But Tom Flannagan was now settled in with all the amenities he'd probably never use: a first-floor convenience store, a library and a room where the residents were allowed to display their own art.

Today, Kate had taken care to wrap the gift purchased at the Gardner and had included a large Hershey bar, which was a favorite. Anything, she thought as her fingers tightened on the wheel, that would make him smile. And for all that he couldn't remember these days, he somehow managed to remember Kate's pain and her divorce. And he'd managed to dredge up a few of Angus's previous flaws with an indelicacy that she'd never heard her father utter.

Today would be different; she wouldn't have to pretend to be happier. She could tell him about her impending date. Give him something different to talk about. She had no problem embellishing if it would help. She just didn't want him to worry. And as she parked the car and went up to his room, she vowed not to say anything about last Saturday and the machinations she'd put herself through. Especially on the day after St. Paddy's...not to her dad. No, he'd want to hear she'd been out having a good time. He'd always pictured celebrating in Boston, but somehow that had never happened, and then her mother died, and of course he'd stopped asking.

With her best smile firmly in place, Kate knocked on her father's door. "He's not so good today," Trudy whispered. "He keeps going on about his house."

"Thanks, Trudy," Kate said as she saw the nurse out. "I'll see what I can do." But she could already see that he was agitated by the way his hands moved and the way his fingertips smoothed over his lips—back and forth—as if he wondered what they were or what they were supposed to do. "It's okay, Dad, the house is in good hands. She knelt beside his chair and kissed his cheek. "I'll drive you over to see it next weekend."

She showed him the cannister, "Would you like some tea; it'll only take a minute. He dismissed the cannister with a sweep of his hand. "I have a date tonight," she said brightly — " isn't it wonderful." He looked relieved if that were even possible. She handed him the chocolate. That calmed him down, which of course was the opposite of what sugar did to her. Bits of chocolate landed on his shirt and that caused him to swipe and swipe until he ground it into the material. "How about I get you a clean T-shirt," she said.

Except for the nurse, his dresser drawers would have been as disjointed as his mind had become. But while she was selecting a clean T-shirt, she spotted a photograph she'd never seen before: a beautiful young woman sitting on a boulder enjoying the sunshine as if she'd been borne to the sea. It wasn't her mother, so it had to be Brigid, she thought before tucking it into her pocket. "Here you go, Dad." Kate handed him the shirt without mentioning the photo.

"Kate?"

"Yes?"

"Is there any more chocolate?"

"I'll bring you more next time, promise, but I have a dinner date, remember and in the meantime, how about I put your favorite program on so that you can keep up with Maine politics."

He smiled, and immediately forgot about the chocolate. Kate kissed him on the top of his head, and on the way out, she filled the night nurse in on what had happened, and emphasized that she wasn't far away, if something came up.

After she left Thornton Oaks, Kate swung by the Curtis Library to see if Maggie's car might still be there. There was no sign of the car, but at least Kate was right on time for her dinner date with Paul.

Chapter 27

1936

October

Dear Diary,
  James is back, exhausted and mean as ever. Or is it because I've gotten used to being fussed over. I've become rather vain, or at least more self-aware than I ever thought was possible, but it's Jake's fault. He says things to me that leave me burning with desire. And wanting to break every one of society's rules. Not to mention God's.
  Jake had been sketching my face until I became comfortable enough to go outside and help him set up a space for what he's decided will be his final work on Hull Island. I won't let myself think about that now, but since he can't possibly paint in the tiny boat cabin, he's talked Helen into letting him paint at her place. I know she still wants to have him around but I'm grateful that she's able to keep an eye on the painting too.
  I'd found some old cloth that I'd intended to use for the table, but he's turned it into a glorious drape that he says brings out the blue in my eyes. And it really does, bluer than I've ever noticed.
  James never mentions my eyes or any of my better qualities, but then he's generally in his cups when he's home and this time is no different.
  Jake has been very careful about keeping his things out of sight just in case, and I found a useable piece of plywood out back that and I lay over the worktable in the attic so there's no evidence of paint. Besides, James still doesn't seem to bother with the attic. I think it is

because he'd rather sit and drink, and fortunately for me, he has returned without the energy required to be bothered with me either.

Tommy is a persistent concern as he wants to jabber away at his father, tell him of all his adventures with Auntie Helen, and I freeze every time I feel James's eyes on me. But then I make light of it, and turn Tommy's attention to Helen's big cat and then he whines that he wants a cat too?

I'm reaching the end of my patience with James, the house, the changing weather which will mean more confinement for me and Tommy. Helen has promised she will take a photograph of the painting the minute it's completed.

I'm signing off now as James is hollering for my company.

Chapter 28

2018

Kate found a parking spot behind the Inn, and walked into the lobby. A fire had been lit and if she hadn't been on a date, she would have plunked her body down in one of the large leather chairs and maybe ordered that martini after all. And once again, she thought how lovely it would be to stay overnight.

As she walked along the corridor, she smelled the famous Noble Burger even before she saw it on a tray carried by a waitress who was about to enter the dining room.

Paul was waiting at the bar, and as soon as he spotted her, he stood and pulled out a stool and as she approached, he leaned in to kiss her on the cheek. "You look nice."

"You do," said the bartender. "What'll you have?"

Kate felt a blush and hoped it wasn't an actual flush as she replied, "A house Chardonnay please."

"He didn't say a thing about me; should I feel insulted?" Paul inquired with a lopsided grin.

"You look nice too," Kate said. "That chestnut color suits you."

"Maggie says it makes me look old."

"I wouldn't worry about looking too mature; you're not even totally gray."

Paul said, "Speaking of mature, how's your father?"

"Thanks for asking," Kate said. "He has early onset Alzheimer's and he keeps wanting to call Senator Collins about some upcoming amendment—don't ask which one. He was not entirely pleased with my gift from the museum, so that's about all I can share, at least until I've had a little wine to help unkink my muscles."

"That has to be tough on you."

"Tougher on him I think, but I'm still learning and maybe so is he in some recess of his mind."

"Then, let's talk about your happy place."

"Ah, yes, the Gardner...what do you want to know."

"More like, would you consider giving me a tour some day?"

"Depends on how well you like flowers, because I'm going back next month for Isabella's birthday celebration on the fourteenth."

"I like flowers, well enough, I guess."

"A tiny history lesson here: the nasturtiums, Isabella's favorites, are strung from the balcony windows in honor of her birthday...isn't that perfect!"

"I guess, but I probably have to see it to form an honest opinion."

Kate wondered just how far her exuberance would get her, just like she wondered if any man would ever 'get' her again, and she said, "If you don't like that idea, we could plan another day, but it would have to be well after the fourteenth."

"Another hot date?"

"I'll never tell," Kate said. "And it looks like our table is ready."

"Do you want one of their burgers," Paul asked as they walked over.

"I've been thinking of it all day," Kate said to their waiter who was standing by. "Make mine medium rare and without the bun, please."

"I'll take mine the same, but with buns and fully dressed," Paul said.

Kate hitched herself up onto one of the stools at the high-top table and placed her jacket over the back, and said, "I've always liked this room, but I wish it was nice enough to sit outside."

"It's Maine, that might not happen for a couple of months."

"But wait ten minutes…"

"The line we all grew up on, but you really do have the most incredible eyes," Paul said. "Now, don't go all red on me; it's true."

"I've recently realized that I don't take compliments very well, so thank you."

"You've been bruised too?"

"What a good word—I was thinking more like bashed, but maybe I would have felt differently if it had been mutual."

"Mine certainly wasn't, but it wasn't due to any infidelity," Paul said. "Sorry, that was insensitive."

"No, I would have been surprised if Maggie hadn't told you.'

"Well, if it makes you feel any better, my divorce wasn't exactly a walk in the park."

"Do we need a refill or can you wing it if I promise to listen attentively?"

Paul raised his hand, and the bartender nodded. "I've helped his mom with her insurance needs, so I get good service in here."

"I don't know if you've noticed, but I also think he may have a thing for you," Kate said.

"I know he does, but it's always been a comfortable joke between us," Paul said under his breath just as their drinks arrived. As soon as the waiter left, he said, "As for my wife, we met after I moved out west and got a job with Humana. We worked hard building our portfolios and gave lip service to starting a family and so on."

"So far, so good," Kate said.

"Then she decided she hated California, hated corporate America, and wanted to move to Montana and open a dude ranch for women."

"Sort of an oxymoron, right?" Kate said.

"Right?" Paul said. "But it wasn't just California that she hated; it was the idea of starting a family. You see, what she hadn't ever told me was that she'd been molested by her father as a girl, and if not for a dear relative who got her some counselling, she might have become pretty promiscuous. Instead, she turned to other girls for solace and did her best to be what she thought was expected of her, until she realized she was living a lie."

"Oh, God," Kate said.

"To her credit, she did try to work things out with us until every argument pushed the walls apart. We lasted a year before I caved and agreed to a divorce."

"Did she fulfill her dream?"

"I never tried to find out; instead, I had an early mid-life crisis and took off for Europe to 'find myself'," Paul said with air quotes that made the waiter take notice.

"Then what?" Kate said.

"Then I came home to Maine and took up with the elderly once again," Paul said. "And here comes our dinner, just in the nick of time before I bore you to tears."

Kate nibbled at her burger, but the thought of what that poor girl would have gone through, and what would happen if women didn't stand up for each other. Suddenly, her mind flew directly to the photo of Brigid that she'd left in her car. *What could have happened all those years ago, and how will I ever know.*

For the next hour and a half, they talked non-stop about their mutual affection for all things Maine, and when the dinner was over, he walked her to her car and kissed her full on the lips before saying goodnight. Her head didn't spin, her heart didn't thump out of her chest; instead, it felt like a lovely bow had been wrapped around her like a Christmas present...special.

They agreed to see each other in town the following week, for lunch at Joshua's Tavern. Only this time, as she waved goodbye, she sensed that her expectations had changed.

Postmortems were important for many things, but maybe not for a date with your best friend's brother, Kate thought as she was back on the Downeaster heading south. She'd had the second date with Paul and it had gone well, but not well enough to continue pretending it could be more than a friendship. Maggie had handled the news better than expected and had come through like a true friend: Paul would join Kate and Maggie for another a dinner, this time at Kate's house at a later date. No harm, no foul, so, all in all, everything would turn out well enough.

Kate looked around at the other passengers and opened a book on Chinese art. This time there was no need to ponder a crime scene and now that she'd dropped ten pounds, she had made peace with her wardrobe too. Plus, the Chanel had been tucked away for occasions other than a return to the Gardner. She felt a strange sense of empowerment that was long overdue.

And when the train pulled into Boston Station, Kate was one of the first to hit the ground with a purpose that defied notice. Let others wonder, she thought as she tucked her phone away in a larger purse and with Angus's number blocked. Ross's card was inside her new black jacket, a soft buttery leather that had already caught the eye of a man with a briefcase and wing tip shoes. He winked and she blushed and walked on, and again thought of Ross and whether or not he'd be at the Gardner again today. Unlike Paul, she'd had a visceral reaction to Ross, a fluttering in her chest that seemed apropos of her cravings, like her newfound interest with her old paintbrushes.

And today, instead of heading for the Cloister, she went up to the second level and stood at her Juliet window and gazed out at the orange garlands strung from the third-floor balconies. Once again, they would not disappoint, but were as glorious as she remembered. If only she could create something memorable, Kate thought as she looked down at the courtyard where necks were craned upward as if they knew she was watching. As far as she could tell, Ross was not among today's interesting mix of museum-goers, but she spotted the couple who'd been on the Downeaster earlier, and she waved. And then, like any carefree traveler without a mission, she sauntered from floor to floor and didn't even check in on dear Rembrandt. Instead, she tried to take in all the wonderful art she had overlooked back in March. And without the distraction of Angus's 'voice', her stress level had lowered and so had her voice when she'd told him in no uncertain terms that she would not meet him and that he had to find someone else to listen to his woes (apparently, the leggy blonde had tired of him).

As the hour slid by, she found herself following a tour group into the Yellow Room and then into the Blue Room where another group stood listening to the guide she'd met back in March. Without distracting her, Kate walked away and went back to the gift shop thinking that it would be lovely to say hi to the girl with the eyebrow jewelry. But then, before she could go inside, her stomach growled fiercely. She had skipped breakfast altogether, and it was now time for lunch. And this time, she intended to stay and have one. Maybe a nice salad to go with her slimmed down waistline. Maybe a nice glass of Prosecco too! After all, this was a day of celebration.

The new wing and Café G were not really new; they'd been there since 2012, but everything felt new today, even her hair which she'd allowed to grow a little longer than usual. As she stood in line waiting to be seated, her eyes darted around the restaurant, and she spotted a face or two among the waitstaff who'd been working there back when she and Angus were a couple. As always, there was a bustle of activity as wines were uncorked and the staff crisscrossed the floor with trays filled with beautiful, modern looking food, as mouthwatering and sumptuous in their simplicity as advertised.

Kate was finally ushered in to a table for one, which was actually for two as they had left it to appear as though she wasn't totally alone. It was the type of thing that indicated they knew their stuff. "I'll have a glass of the Acinum Prosecco," she said to a waiter who didn't seem old enough to drink. "Have you been here long," she asked.

"My first week," "but I've wanted to work here ever since I can remember."

"Wow, good for you," Kate replied.

"My Gran used to bring me here for the nasturtiums"

"That's why I'm here today, and I wish you the best of luck doing what you love."

He smiled and left her to ponder the other diners to her heart's content. And then another staffer dropped off a creamy burrata salad that was tailormade for today though she watched the door just in case. And then she yawned…from the alcohol no less, but as soon as she paid the bill, she headed for the courtyard to have one more glimpse of the garlands before leaving for home.

She found a spot in between two pillars. The garlands, the color of marmalade, glistened as if they'd been dipped in sunshine. Suddenly, someone tapped her on the shoulder and she was so startled, she whipped around and nearly tripped over her own feet. "Hi," Ross said as if running into her here was an everyday occurrence.

"Hi."

"Did you enjoy your lunch?"

"How did you know I was there?"

"I spotted you as I was leaving to catch up with a business acquaintance, and then circled back and you were gone."

"Well, I guess you've found me, then."

"Can I interest you in a glass of wine?"

"Not wine, but I think I could use a coffee."

They walked out of the garden as if they'd always taken a stroll together, neither one saying very much, just a comfortable sharing of space. And when they reached the Café, he led her to a table marked 'reserved'. This must be where he conducts business, she thought, and it did have an excellent view of the outside garden path. "Let me say, you look much happier than the last time I saw you, brief as it was."

"I am happier, and especially since I made the effort to come back today," Kate said. "It's always been something special, and I haven't exactly had the courage to face the things that I used to enjoy, especially here."

"Courage?"

Why not lay it out there, she thought; time was short and who knew when or if she'd ever see him again. "Long story short, I met my husband here, and we've recently divorced, and I was afraid to face all the memories."

"And now?"

"Now I feel like a new and better version of that woman, and plan to make the trip down from Maine often."

"Maine, no kidding, whereabouts?

She noted that his posture had changed as soon as she'd mentioned Maine. She said, "Hull Island; do you know it?"

"This is uncanny; my grandfather was raised on the Boothbay Peninsula and we used to go to Hull when I was a kid, during my summer vacations. Absolutely the best summers of my life," Ross said. "He loved it so much that when he retired, he and my grandmother bought a house there."

"You've got to be kidding; where?" Kate said.

"It's on Lupine Lane about three miles from Cove's End."

"I have a friend who lives on Cove's End," Kate said while watching the way his eyes danced.

"He's been gone awhile but before my gran died, she deeded their house to me, and I turned it into a rental since I was working out of Boston. And oddly enough, I decided to stop renting and keep it for myself."

Kate sat in disbelief and said, "So, do you live there or here."

"Both, I guess. I go up there when I need to get away from the city, but suddenly I'm inclined to think I might have to make some adjustments, now that I know you're there."

"Are you so certain that I will be waiting for you?" Kate said, even though something told her that she would be.

"I'm taking a big risk here, Kate, but I think we both felt something when we bumped into each other that first time."

"I can't promise anything, but I'll give you my number in case you ever do come up, and we'll see."

"What more could a guy ask, except maybe a quick swing-through of my favorite spot in the entire museum."

"And where is that?"

"The Raphael Room; that is if you have time."

"Tell me what you love about that gallery."

"Majesty and romance, all combined into one space; haven't you ever wanted to sit in front of that fireplace and wile away an hour daydreaming of what it must have been like during his time, because I have," Ross said. "I don't have an artistic bone in my body, but I love the Renaissance painters, and I'm guessing you have found your own favorites or you wouldn't keep coming back."

Kate studied his face and the boyish exuberance in his words, never once thinking she could have come across someone with a shared passion for both the museum and her island. And of course, she wouldn't have if Angus hadn't left her. "I am partial to Rembrandt if you must know, but there is a very long history of time spent with *El Jaleo*, which I don't have hours enough to explain right now.

"But I do have just enough time before I have to catch my train to pop in on Raphael if you like."

They left immediately and strode through the corridor without actually touching, but close enough had they wanted to. Once inside the gallery on the second floor, Kate expelled a long breath; she hadn't seen this room in years. "So gorgeous!"

"Like you," Ross said as he looked deeply into her eyes. "You look like you belong in a Renaissance painting."

"Now you are going too far."

"Nonsense...but if it makes you uncomfortable, I'll save my compliments until we know each other a little better."

They lingered a few minutes longer and then she turned and said, "Ross, I'm really flattered, honestly, but I can't promise anything right now. I've worked through my divorce well enough, but I don't know if I'm ready to get involved in another relationship...and given our distances, that might be a difficult thing to do."

"Why not let me worry about that part for now; just promise me you will answer my calls, because I *will* call you, and we'll take it from there."

What could she say…he was the total package; it just depended on whether or not the packaging was of good quality, she thought as she gazed into his eyes. "I really do have to run now; you stay here and enjoy the room while I make a dash for my train."

Kate left him standing there in front of the fireplace, and in the midst of all that solid wood furniture that had stood the test of time. "Wouldn't it be grand if one man could do the same," she whispered to herself.

Chapter 29

1937

Dear Diary,

I haven't written since before the holidays; so much has happened. Helen and Tommy and I celebrated with Mrs. Budreau and Helen's cat who she'd dressed in a little red bib. James left unexpectedly, gone off to make another fortune that I would never see. We lit a candle for his safe return, the way I had taught Tommy to do, but my own heart had already seized over.

On top of that Jake finished the painting ahead of schedule and then went off to Monhegan again because he believed that I would be with James. Everything seems a mess now but I managed to sneak a look at the painting that she'd hidden away for me, and I couldn't believe my eyes. Jake had taken his sketches of her and managed to include Helen so that we would have this memory of our friendship forever. And if James ever did see it, at least I wouldn't be seen as posing alone and just maybe he'd think twice before raising a hand to me.

The painting is better than expected, I'm in a dreamscape that is my own backyard, and Helen is gazing up while I'm gazing at Jake; it's so perfect and I want so badly to hang it in my house, but of course I can't.

And just when I thought everything would be okay when Jake returned, James came home early and carrying a sack that Tommy mistook for Santa's bag, and when he didn't find any toys, he flew into a tantrum. James blamed me yet again for spoiling him.

While James was over in Harpswell, I took Tommy to the kiddy park. It was the only place I could think of where Jake could show up unnoticed. Stupid me, the kids rushed to him because he was new and different and carrying the satchel he was never without, which was like a magnet to the children. They rushed him, and jabbered about what they wanted for Christmas and he just smiled and nodded. Fortunately, he didn't try to win them over with his mastery of the English language or all of their parents would have found a way to tie us together with the gossip that I know has begun to spread.

But Jake had a surprise for me inside the satchel, a drawing of a shingled cabin that he wants to buy just for 'us'. But I don't dare dream of such a thing.

Then, we got careless because I didn't know that James had come back and was out working on Lady Dora's rigging. Thankfully, I had dropped Tommy at Helen's because Jake barely made it out through the front door just as James was coming in through the back because he'd forgotten one of his tools. Or so he said. Now I'm wondering if he made up going to Harpswell just so he could catch me off guard. No matter, it was a very close call. And now I have to go retrieve Tommy and start dinner as though nothing ever happened.

Helen came back with me as a buffer, saying that she'd made a pie for our dinner and Tommy had already started to doze in my arms. I'm not sure how much James believes, but I can tell that she is beginning to tire of my little escapades. How can I blame her. She had such high hopes for a new man in her life, and my involvement with Jake has turned her a little bitter even though she tries to hide it.

"How can I truly trust someone so in love with the same man?"

Chapter 30

2018

Kate stepped off the train at Brunswick Station. And unlike the month before, today's sky was as still and bespoke as a deep-blue pinstriped suit. The air smelled of earth and food that had been grilled out behind someone's house or maybe it was from the outdoor terrace at the Inn. There was a scent of promise in the air too, and it was as bold as anything Maine had to offer at this time of year. But the concept of losing her head over what might or might not happen with Ross, was barely digestible, no matter the season. She was afraid of course; this strange sensation might fizzle out before she could reach her cottage or he might have forgotten her the moment he left the museum. And by the time she had run the gamut of emotions, she realized she was already parked in her driveway and her initial excitement hadn't gone away. The unfamiliarity of such a thing, made her want to share the news, but was it too soon to be heralding another man after what had happened with Maggie's brother. Or would Maggie be the least judgmental of anyone, given their history, which meant that she called her the moment she was through the door. As expected, it went to voicemail, but Kate invited her to stop by on her way home from the library and then she made sure she had some of Maggie's favorite wine on hand. She even took some care that there was something to cook for dinner in case whatever they hashed out, could be sustained with at least some protein.

At precisely six, the door knocker banged...aggressive, but not angrily. Kate walked to the door and opened it to find

Maggie standing there with a bottle of Kate's favorite red and a batch of flowers that had come from the grocery store. "You must have had a good day," Kate said.

"You wouldn't believe how much I accomplished, and from the sound of your voice, I'm guessing that you also had a banner day. And before you say anything, if it has to do with that business card you showed me, you deserve whatever you want…no hard feelings about Paul—at all."

Kate hugged her tight enough to make her squeal, and said, "Thank you, I needed that; now come on into the kitchen and get comfortable while I open this and then I'll tell you everything."

"Shoot," Maggie said as she settled into one of Kate's painted chairs.

"It was such a good day, I don't know where to begin, but I got to see the nasturtiums which were amazing by the way, and then I followed a guided tour for a few minutes…"

"Not that, the good parts," Maggie said.

"Ross, who, by the way, is still gorgeous, was there too; not that I believed for a minute that I'd see him again. But he spotted me while I was having lunch at the Café, and after he'd finished up with some sort of meeting, he came and found me outside in the courtyard."

"And?"

"And we went back to the Café for a coffee, and that's when he started coming on and strong, at least for me," Kate said. "But I felt something, really, and not just because he thinks I'm beautiful, which was a total come-on, but because he loves that place almost as much as I do. But then he dropped a total bombshell; he actually has a little place, here on the island, can you believe it?"

"Wow, how'd that happen?"

"It's a house he inherited from his grandparents."

"So now what?"

"Now I wait and see if he'll call like he said, and if he does, then I don't know."

"You've had quite a day for a girl new to the dating game," Maggie said. "You don't suppose I could talk you into a bit of online dating now too?"

"I'm considering it; after all, Ross may never call, but he made me feel like I'm no longer a wallflower waiting for someone to ask me to dance."

"That's the spirit," Maggie said as she pulled her phone out of her sweater pocket. "This is the latest dating app, and a very smart one it is."

They spent the rest of the evening looking at photos and while pouring out their highs and lows of the day, they managed to pour all the wine too. "That was delicious," Maggie said.

"Just what I like to call my 'clean out the fridge quiche'," Kate said. "And my empty shelves are proof of it."

"Before I go on, I want you to know that I spoke with Paul again, and he's fine, really. I sensed he was relieved because you both had a similar reaction, *and* he's already asked a woman from his bank out on a date, so now we can all move forward."

"He's such a nice man, and he's your brother, and I wanted it to work, really, but it isn't meant to be."

"That's the whole point; it has to feel right, but we three will continue to have the occasional meal together and air our grievances and share our accomplishments."

"How'd you get so darn wise?" Kate asked.

"Trial and error, my friend, and a lot of stumbling over myself while trying."

Chapter 31

1937

Dear Diary,

It's been a week, but James is still angry with me though he hasn't come out and said anything specific. He can't prove I've been seeing Jake behind his back, there's nothing of him anywhere in the house that James could find, particularly if he sticks to his regular routines. But tongues are wagging, that's for sure.

Thankfully, the winter is still mild and I was able to take Tommy to the park again so he could see his friend, Carla, who is four. Jake was there again too, this time with a few pages of the plans he's worked out for the cabin he wants to build on Monhegan that he'd rolled and put into some kind of tube with straps that he'd flung over his shoulder. Of course, that gave him an air of mystery. Thankfully, the little kids were busy with their own games this time but I'm still worried about what will come out of Tommy's mouth if he's questioned.

James is worried about the weather; the rigging ices over when the storms blow up and they do that without warning. I should be worried because he's due to leave in two days. But I'm more worried that I have to make a decision. Helen says that running away with the man as she herself would have done, would mark me for life, and there again, what of Tommy?

But each time she says things like that, I worry that she is planning on betraying me. She claims she has her eye on a man who knew her brother, but that doesn't ring true. I never, ever thought I'd be the one to steal Jake's heart, and now I wouldn't know how to give it back.

Chapter 32

2018

Summer was already knocking on the door, and the birds in Kate's yard converged with joy on both their birdbaths: wash, rinse, and repeat. Kate blamed a lot of her behavior on the worst case of spring fever she'd ever known. Romantic notions shattered her dreams and had her waking in delicious quivers. Ross had called, twice, and had resolved to come up from Boston the very next weekend. Instead of a train to Brunswick, where she might have been obligated to pick him up, he would drive up and stay at his cottage, and she'd had kept her feelings to herself. Excitement was one thing, spring fever as she knew it, was another, and the between-the-sheets type of intimacy might take a little longer. He had told her quite a lot about himself during their lengthy phone conversations: his parents had divorced and his mother now lived in Connecticut with a man who treated her like royalty. While on the other hand, his father had disappeared into the bowels of a Vegas hotel where the only standards were that he had to wear a clean shirt every day or else.

Ross had gone on to explain that before his grandparents had moved to Hull Island, he'd been able to continue on at school in Boothbay Harbor by being allowed to live with them full time. Kate had read between the lines when Ross modestly mentioned his track medals. Of course, Kate had thought at the time, his body appeared that sinewy even in a suit. But for all of that, Kate could tell that Ross was holding back something. He'd never married, which was a red flag according to Maggie, who had already helped Kate to sign up for a membership in some over-fifty group online. Maggie was then tasked with all the sorting out because that sort of thing was her personal forte.

Kate still had trepidations about meeting someone in that way—all that swiping back and forth seemed so childish—but Maggie had just met a man she thought might be 'the one who would dance like no one was watching', or so she'd said.

Kate desperately wanted happiness for her friend, but she thought of herself as more of a target for ridicule: her hair had taken a rebellious turn just when Maggie needed photos to submit on her behalf. And Kate's 'elevens' had become even more prominent in the past month, or maybe that was just the frown that came from squinting at the dating app.

A few days later, Kate received a call from the head nurse at Thornton who'd said that her father had been crying a lot lately and would Kate see if she could find out what was troubling him. He'd already begun to degrade physically, and would be moved to another wing soon.

The grounds around the buildings had begun to fill in with plants that were highlighted with the colors of a deepening sky. It was another matter on the second floor where she found her father sitting behind drapes that had been pulled tight. Kate walked in and immediately opened them. "Look Dad, it's like a nighttime rainbow out there."

Her voice had startled him from wherever he'd traveled, and he began to cry.

"Don't cry Dad, please."

"I miss my mother; where did she go?"

"Oh, Dad, Gran's been gone a long time; don't you remember, she went away when you were just a boy and you and your father took a trip together...he even let you steer the big boat. Then you spent the summer with someone you called auntie Helen."

"No!"

"Yes, Dad, and when you went back to your own house for the school year, Grandad had fixed up your room with toy boats and that's when you decided to be a fisherman when you grew up."

"I did," Tom said with clarity at last. "But how did you know?"

"Mum told me; you just forgot, and now you feel better, right?"

"Kate, I miss your mother."

"Me too, Dad, me too," Kate said. "Is there any chance you remember more about Brigid?"

"So pretty...the sailors always whistled when she took me down to see the boats, and Dad was always mad at her, but not me. I loved her, even when the kids teased me, I stuck up for her."

"Do you know why they teased you, Dad?"

"Said she was cheating, but Mum never played card games or croquet or anything, so I never knew why they said that."

"Do you remember a man who might have done a painting of Gran?"

"No!"

"Are you sure, Dad, maybe he had a mustache or a funny hat?"

"He made a picture of her and I hid it away."

"When, Dad, when did you do that?"

"When I grew up, of course."

Kate could already see the strain on his face; she had pushed him too far, but oh how close she was to finding out the truth—at least she had the photo. "I'll come back tomorrow, Dad, you get some rest now, okay?"

"Rest, yes, I need rest, but you forgot my chocolate."

"I left it with the nurse; she'll give it to you for desert tonight," Kate said as she was about to leave. "Don't worry, Dad, we'll sort this all out, I promise."

"Women don't keep promises," he yelled; it was her cue to leave.

When Kate returned home, there was a message from Maggie stating that she'd found someone on a spanking new dating app, a man she wanted Kate to see. In order to do that Kate had to pull out her cellphone and punch in the password so she could scroll until she found the 'handle': NO GAMES, PLEASE. She giggled; what a silly name, and yet, he was attractive and the bio had an appealing ring. "No one wants to play games at this stage in life," Kate said to Maggie who had waited on the land line. "Okay, now what?"

"You tap one of those emojis to indicate your interest and see what happens next."

"Just like that."

"Easy as pie; he will be interested in you or not, and we'll take it from there."

"We, is right; I'm not doing this all by myself," Kate said. "And I'm not sure I'm doing it at all."

"Fine; so how was your dad?"

"Not good, and you remember that painting of Gran, well he rambled on and now I'm sure something has happened to it, and I have to find it."

"Can I help in any way?"

"Thanks, but let me think first. I don't even know what needs to be done, but I'll get back to you."

"Talk soon, then," Maggie said as she hung up.

Kate spent all of Sunday sorting and cleaning, and when she was satisfied, she pulled out her mother's recipe book and decided to make a roast pork that would be easy to live off for the next few days, which would leave her time to concentrate on more important things.

While the scent of pork filled the house, Kate thumbed through her latest novel. It was a mystery, very different from the one of Agatha's, and the protagonist was far older than Kate, which made for an interesting plot line.

But the thing that drew Kate in, was that in this novel, the protagonist had snooped around and found her daughter's diary. What if her own mother had found a diary, Kate thought. Hiding one in that old house was highly plausible and there had been those snippets of conversation that she'd been too young to put into context. And those colors in the attic had meant something had gone on. And dear Mary Flannagan used to snoop through Kate's drawers when she was a teenager, so who knows what she might have discovered from Brigid's belongings.

But now what, Kate wondered, it wasn't in with all the things she'd brought to the cottage when she moved in.

She shouted at her novel, "It's got to be in storage!"

"I'm heading for the storage locker," Kate said as soon as Maggie picked up the phone.

"Want me to go with?"

"Thanks, but I can manage; I'll call if I find what I'm looking for."

"Fingers crossed," Maggie said.

"Love you," Kate said as she hung up.

Unit thirty-two was at the end of a long corridor, the padlock still bright and brassy looking: no burglars allowed. Not that anyone would be interested in her old stuff, but there was one slim chest of drawers thought to be of value that she'd hung onto, just in case.

Hunting through her mother's things brought up feelings that went beyond sadness. As far as Kate was concerned, Mary Flannagan was an enigma who had been put on this earth to keep everyone else on their toes. And now Kate was untethered from that life, not only by her mother's death, but because of the discourse and commitment to family that was no longer available.

Kate peered into the unit without knowing where to even begin and before she could, it was necessary to remove the old worn quilts she'd used as a covering on the larger pieces of furniture. There was very little saved from her life in Boston, but she refused to get rid of certain pieces that had come from the Hull Island house when her father moved to Thornton.

Once everything was uncovered, she found the chest of drawers from her parents' bedroom, and remembered the times she'd put her tiny fingers into the ring pulls only to find that nothing happened. Now, she did the same but with so much more strength that the drawers squealed as if they were in pain. If only she'd brought a bar of soap, she thought as she struggled until all six drawers were opened. Sadly, they were all empty.

After a poor attempt at closing them, she slipped between an old rocker and the chest of drawers that had been in her childhood bedroom. The same thing happened with its drawers, and again, they were empty.

The movers had left her just enough space between the pieces of furniture and various boxes that contained her mother's best Sunday dishes and a particular pot for stews that Kate never prepared, but there was also a round box on top of a stack of sweater boxes. She would come back for those once October was in the rearview mirror. As she was placing the sweater box back in place, her shin hit something rough and scratchy, which turned out to be the edge of a very old pie chest. Chests like this came in different sizes and types of wood and hers was painted pine with a mesh-front door that allowed for air flow. It was too beloved to sell and too big to put in her own kitchen and she hadn't peeked inside it for many years.

She bent over and rubbed her leg and noticed that the door was slightly off its hinges and wasn't sure if moving it had made it that way or not. She turned the small knob and opened the door on the left, which is where the flour would have been stored. Then she opened the side with shelving and saw that her mother's old sewing kit, a round metal container with a tray inside was front and center.

The movers had to have put it there so that it wouldn't be lost in transit. But the tray had packs of needles, a cloth measuring tape and a pencil. Kate lifted the tray to find a pair of pinking shears and a packet of letters tied with a frayed ribbon as if it had been tied and retied many times. Love letters, she thought, but refused to read as if it would be prying now that she couldn't share them with her father.

Instead, she took them over to her sweater box, saving their words for cold winter nights when she needed that type of solace, when she felt the most alone, the way she'd felt this past winter.

She walked back to the pie chest to close it and cover it up when she saw a tea towel shoved way in back that had been wrapped around something solid. And as soon as she unwrapped the towel, the air suddenly filled with the scent of old age instead of old wood.

An honest to goodness diary, she thought as she tried the lock with her fingernail. But it needed something stronger, so she got the scissors from the sewing box and pried the lock while being mindful not to destroy the ancient metal clasp.

She sneezed as the yellowed pages were exposed, but unlike the smell, the words were crisp and clear. Now she couldn't wait to get home and instead of recovering the furniture, she fled to the corridor, pulled the door down behind her, and put the padlock back in place.

Then she ran out to her car, opened the window, and snapped on the light. Her breathing normalized from the fresh air and she pleaded: "Please let it be." But even as she whispered the words, she knew that it felt wrong to read the diary in the car. Her grandmother's words merited more attention — the light of day or candlelight and a glass of wine, and music, something soft and kind, the way any woman wanted to be treated.

Kate laid the diary on the passenger seat and started the car. She had never had a speeding ticket and this might end her perfect record, but as she thought about what this might mean to her and to her father, she really didn't care.

Once she was within the safe bounds of her driveway, she let out the breath she'd been holding in. And then she sneezed. The diary was going to make for quite a challenge no matter how she accompanied her reading, but she rushed inside and as she tugged off her jacket, she ignored the blinking red button on her answering machine and went straight to the kitchen. She placed the diary on the table and looked at the roast that she'd left out on the counter. It had long cooled down but the aroma still filled the kitchen in the way that her mother's meatloaf had done. Kate looked at the pork, glistening in its juices and her stomach growled, and like a greedy child, she pulled at it with her fingers, remembering the loving tap she would always receive for having bad manners. Then, she poured herself a glass of the white wine that had been left in the fridge and decided to slip into something more comfortable, snapping on the radio as she went to her bedroom.

It was only a diary, but it was *her* diary, Kate thought knowing what the truth might mean. While she'd been changing, she pictured the perfect spot to read Brigid's words: the leather reading chair that she had rescued from the old attic when the Hull Island house had been sold. She often read in bed instead of sitting with her memories in 'old man' Flannagan's chair, but not tonight. She knew it was unreasonable since it was a perfectly comfortable, in fact, a highly comfortable chair even with its wear and tear and a spring that had to be sat on just so. But James had been responsible for many of the words that had been hurled through her childhood home, and so she'd chosen the small wing chair instead or on the floor with her back against the sofa and her feet on the cocktail table while she watched TV.

This evening would be different; the choice of chair defiant, and the hurricane lamp, a nostalgic touch. And suddenly, she laughed. By going back to the Gardner, she was again channeling her inner romantic, and this felt especially good now that she had sidelined Angus's attempts to wriggle his way back into her life.

And as she realized how freeing it was to be on solid footing again, she opened Brigid's diary.

An hour later, Kate had read each entry and then gone back and read them all over again. And before the night was out, she would probably read it one more time. The problem was that it was incomplete, which meant she had to imagine what was happening and that led to filling in the blanks with her own feelings.

There were water marks on a few of the pages, which Kate surmised had been from her grandmother's tears. And each page became as important to her as Mary Flannigan's Holy Bible, which Kate had kept in her possession since her mother's death.

Now Kate gave thanks that her mother had been savvy enough to keep Brigid's diary through thick and thin, even though the contents must have made her blood boil. Adultery was not to be taken lightly in the Flannagan household, and again, Kate was grateful that Angus's misdeeds had not happened on her mother's watch.

Kate went back to the kitchen and poured a second glass of wine and sat down to fix herself a sandwich before putting the pork in the fridge. Then, she picked up the phone. "Please come," she said before Maggie could say anything at all.

Ten minutes later, Maggie marched in through the back door—without knocking—and said, "See, I'm capable of overcoming my fear of the creepies in the trees."

"You aren't, but you braved it for me, and I appreciate it."

"Is this what you were looking for in the storage unit," Maggie asked as she pulled a stool over to the leather chair.

"It is and I'm so sad. It's incomplete, and maybe that's because she'd run out of time. But look at this last entry before you read anything and tell me what you think.

"James is drunk, worse than usual, I think he's going to kill me and bury me out to sea," Maggie read. "You don't think he did, do you?"

"It would explain a lot," Kate said. "He was a real bastard and from what I read, she had a horrific marriage."

"Here, let me see the rest." Maggie carefully pried open the pages, and quietly mouthed a few lines. "Outrageous! It's not only a sad commentary on the times, but how could she not do what she was threatening to do, the man was evil!"

Kate took the diary back and opened it to an entry about Monhegan Island. "This hints that she was about to run away, and I don't blame her, but think of my poor dad and how that must have impacted his entire childhood."

"But what if she didn't run away, but was taken away with no one the wiser?"

"I can't bear to think of that, Maggie, I really can't. We're talking about my dad's father here."

"I know and I'm sorry, but you can't say the thought hasn't crossed your mind."

"Maybe that's why my parents never said much," Kate offered. "But I just can't believe she would leave my dad behind."

"I get that, but maybe James threw her out and she had no choice but to run away with Jake, not much easier to swallow since she obviously left your dad behind anyway," Maggie said.

"It's just too awful to even imagine what Dad must have gone through and let me tell you, I'm not at all proud to be related to James Flannagan."

"And here's another mention of someone named Helen," Maggie said. "It says she took the photo; maybe she kept the painting?"

"I wonder if she really did throw my gran under the bus."

"Too many entries are missing," Maggie said.

"If only I had a way of getting back inside the old house; maybe there's something still hidden away in there."

"Seems unlikely and if there had been, it would have been tossed out as junk by now. I threw most everything away that had been left by the previous owner after I moved into my cottage. Who wants someone else's memories lying around."

"Me, of course, but only because I know what they mean."

"Too bad there isn't someone like Jake on one of the apps," Maggie said.

"Right, that's all I need right now, some overzealous guy trying to get me into bed while he probably has another lover stashed over on Monhegan Island."

"That is just like you, blowing it all out of proportion; the guy may or may not have been a lothario waiting for her husband to crash and burn; he might have fallen madly in love with Brigid," Maggie said. "And he might have been devasted at losing her, however that may have occurred; they're not all like Angus."

"You're right, and to think that just a couple of hours ago, I was actually leaning on the precipice of romantic notions," Kate said. "Go figure."

"Thata girl!"

"Would you like some leftover pork to take home?"

"Yes, please," Maggie said as she followed Kate into the kitchen.

Chapter 33

Kate finished cleaning up the kitchen all the while thinking of what Maggie had said about the man who may have truly loved Brigid. Isn't that what we all want, Kate thought as she went into her bedroom. It broke her heart to think of how badly her grandmother had been treated and her anger extended to the great-grandparents who were so misinformed about a woman's rights and needs. Kate was filled with gratitude; she'd been loved in a way that allowed her to feel cherished. And with her mother gone, she could feed off that love even more. And more than anything, she hoped to bring some peace to her father, though she hardly knew what that would entail in his present state of mind.

Placing the diary on her nightstand to read again in the morning, she mentally organized her work calendar; she hoped to return to Thornton Oaks sometime in the late afternoon on Monday. And if there was enough time, to swing by the old homestead and do a little snooping about. And maybe if she got lucky, have a nice chat with the new owners, hopefully Mainers since they would probably invite her in, maybe give her a tour of any changes to the interior they'd made, and maybe she'd mention the sea captain and spark their interest in the lore of the captain's house.

They wouldn't need to know the gritty details, just that he'd been a hardboiled seaman who'd taken a hard right when he should have swung left during a turbulent nor'easter. If the new owners seemed interested enough, she might tell them that the *Lady Dora* rested at the bottom of the Atlantic with five souls on board and that Kate would dearly love to find a small memento that might have been left behind in her childhood home. Of course, with what Maggie had hinted at, there may have been six souls and that would have to be kept from her father.

Monday proved busier than she'd expected and now she was rushing through traffic and of course, hitting every red light possible. She was counting on the fact that the nurse often took her father for a walk around the property after he'd had his dinner, which would give her just enough time to take one last look through his apartment.

Kate knocked and when no one answered, she let herself in and immediately went to his bedroom, which was darker than it needed to be. Her father had been in a holding pattern lately and one of the things that could upset him was too much light. Kate turned on the bedside lamps and began to look through his closet: coat pockets, the few items on the top shelf, and even the inside of his shoes. Nothing.

Nothing in the dresser drawers either and then she remembered the suitcase that he insisted be placed under his bed, stating that he would need it when he left, which he also insisted would be the next day, no matter when she visited.

Opening the suitcase brought on the tears she'd kept in check whenever he was near. This entire chapter in his life broke her heart; the man she'd known all her life was slowly disappearing. How was she supposed to understand his replacement.

He'd always been larger than life, though not necessarily in stature. Fair and loving and stern when he thought it necessary, but now there was a bitterness seeping through, and fear. He'd never been afraid, not even the time he'd gone overboard and flailed about while she frantically threw him a life preserver.

Her sainted mother must be rolling in her grave, Kate thought as she closed the suitcase and double-checked the time. Then she went to the living room and began scouring the shelves that were still filled with books that she supposed he'd never read. There were no indications that any of them had been touched since she was last in the apartment.

And nothing that even smelled of long-ago pages that he might have ripped from a diary out of anger without thinking of the consequences. No manilla folders or envelopes tucked out of sight from a nurse's prying eyes by someone who had become paranoid of late.

Kate moved from the shelves to the cupboards beneath the TV stand—still nothing. She worried that she was missing some component to the Flannagan story, but without her father's ability to guide her, she would never learn what that was.

Suddenly, she heard her father's voice in the hall and she rose from her knees and walked to the door in time to hear him knock. It was as if he didn't realize he lived inside and then she heard the nurse's voice.

Kate opened the door, and said, "I was wondering when you'd come back."

Her father looked at her as if he had no idea who she was. She flinched, but she bit back the tears, and said, "Don't worry, Dad, I just came by with more chocolates."

"Kate?"

"Yep, that's me."

"My girl, you've grown up and you're so pretty."

Her heart could not be any more broken, she thought, but instead, she smiled at the man whom she had loved all her life and said, "Mom always told me you liked this color so I'm wearing blue just for you, Dad."

"That's my girl, but I'm tired now; see you in the morning."

And with that, the nurse on duty—Janice this time—took him by the elbow and escorted him to the darkened bedroom.

Kate listened at the door, grateful he had such caring women to get him through his days and nights when she had no clue how to cope.

She waited until Janice returned to the living room, and said, "Thank you from the bottom of my heart."

"He's going to be all right, dear, go home and get some rest."

Kate had nothing left to give strangers who occupied the world she had known all her life, nothing but sadness now. Her father would never be the same, she would never know the entire story of Brigid's life and that was all there was to it.

And by the time she arrived home she was totally spent, that is, until she saw a message from Ross saying to call him back because he had a surprise. "What's up," Kate said though her heart was weeping still.

"How about we take a day trip to Monhegan Island on Saturday?"

"Really!" A surge of adrenalin along with some strange kind of hopefulness hit her. "Ooh that would be wonderful; I haven't been in years."

"I can drive up on Friday night, and yes, I plan to stay at my place in case you were wondering."

"I think both things are a great idea, Ross."

"Terrific, I'll pick you up at six forty-five; I've made reservations on the *Balmy Days*. That'll give us a couple of hours to hike around Monhegan and when we get back, we can have dinner in Boothbay Harbor."

"Wow, what a great idea." Kate loved the fact that he was allowing for quality time to get to know one another instead of just trying to get her into bed, which is what she'd half expected. No matter how suave or handsome he was, he was still a single man looking for love or whatever else he'd need. Then again, as Maggie had said, *not all men are like Angus.*

"I kinda thought so myself," Ross said. "I'll call you when I arrive Friday night and we can hash out any last-minute ideas."

"Perfect," Kate said although against all restraint, her insides were filled with butterflies and not a few trepidations. Was she fit enough for those trails; did she even have a small backpack or did Maggie. "Talk soon, then."

After the line went dead, Kate picked up her cell so that she could walk around while she talked to Maggie. "Do you have a backpack I can borrow?" Kate said taking their conversation into her bedroom.

"What on earth for?"

"Ross is taking me to Monhegan next Saturday and I need to be prepared."

"Are you sure you're okay about this date," Maggie said. "What aren't you telling me?"

"Just stuff pertaining to my dad; he barely knows me anymore, and I doubt I'll ever find out what happened to Brigid, but yes, I'm good with the date because it'll help take my mind off everything else."

"Are you trying to convince me or yourself?"

"Both. But at least Ross has his own place and thereby removing my own anxiety."

"That's a good thing, and in the meantime, don't forget we're meeting Paul for drinks Thursday," Maggie said.

"I did actually…so how about you guys come here and I'll wrestle up something tasty and we can hash out whatever we need to without fuss or muss," Kate said.

"Is there anything I can do for you, anything I can say about your dad that will make you feel better," Maggie said. "You don't have to go this alone you know?"

"I know, but I think just being there for me is enough."

"I am here for whatever, and speaking of, what can I bring over on Thursday?"

"How about some of that wonderful French bread," Kate said. "And I think it's about time I show Paul that photo I didn't bring over to your place that first time."

"We'll be there at six," Maggie said.

Chapter 34

The rain pelted the roof and lashed against the windows. Kate put on her best face and fixed her hair, already unruly from the damp, and added to by poking her head in the oven to check on the ziti. But the entire house now smelled like the kitchen; oregano, thyme, basil, and a pinch of cinnamon. And the cheese bubbling over the top: the finest Grana Padano she'd ever been able to buy.

She had left the door unlocked and even though they knocked, Maggie and Paul entered before she was able to reach the front door. Paul whistled. "This is a great space!"

"I like it."

"She's done amazing things with this place," Maggie said. "You should have seen it before she became addicted to paint."

"Don't listen to her, Paul, the kitchen is the only room where I went a little crazy with color, but I do like the pale fern shade for this room," Kate said. "And it does wonders for my spirit during the winter."

"Smart gal," Paul said. "Maybe I should hire you as my decorator."

"No flirting, remember," Maggie said.

"Here we go again," Kate said as she ushered them into the kitchen and handed each a glass of wine.

"I see what you meant about the kitchen," Paul said shielding his eyes as if the glare was too much. "And the wine is a great choice too."

"It's become a favorite of your sister's...she calls it *precocious!*"

Winking, he said. "Does she now?"

"We have a few minutes before dinner's ready, and Paul, I need to show you something first," Kate said as she picked up the photo from the sideboard.

Paul pointed to the polished wood that had been underneath the photo, and said, "That's a beauty."

"Just another of my DIY projects, but I think I did a pretty good job patching it up," Kate said as she handed him the photo. "But the sanding was a bitch."

Paul ran his hand over the surface and said, "Smooth as a baby's bottom".

"What would you know about babies," Maggie said.

"I seem to recall helping to change your nasty diaper once upon a time."

"Children, please!" Kate said knowing that this could go on longer than she had time for tonight.

"Sorry," Paul said as he batted Maggie's hand away, and then he looked at the photograph, a quizzical expression on his face.

"What's wrong?" Kate said.

He looked up at her and then back at the photo, and said, "I know this isn't you, but I also know that I have actually seen this painting somewhere before now."

"Impossible!" Maggie yelped.

"No! I'm telling you; this was somewhere in Boothbay or thereabouts—the home of one of my elderly clients; I'm sure of it."

"Is there some way we can find out who?" Kate said just as the oven timer dinged.

"I'd need to go through my computer files, which isn't a huge job, but it's the only way to see if any names ring any sort of bell," Paul said. "That's the best I can do."

"Do better than that, brother dear; it's a matter of urgency," Maggie said.

"Don't hit me," Paul said as he reached for the breadboard and the knife.

Chapter 35

Kate tossed and turned. The baked ziti had been such a huge success that she'd had seconds. It had been so easy to overeat with Paul taking the helm and steering their conversation towards all things hysterical about growing up with Maggie.

But now Kate was so wound, she couldn't sleep. The thought of the painting actually being out there and possibly so close by was mind-boggling. Paul would try, she was certain, and maybe they'd get lucky; just the thought of being able to bring it home to Hull Island where it had always belonged made her want to weep from joy.

"Oh God, it's nearly Friday," she said to the clock on the nightstand. Tomorrow she would look like hell; there had to be a way to shut off her brain. The rain had stopped right after dinner and now Kate rolled over onto her right side and looked out at a sinking moon...this had been some week!

She must have dozed at some point, because when the alarm went off, she practically fell out of bed. She'd been dreaming about a watercolor of a mermaid and the clock said that she'd gotten three whole hours of sleep. And now she had to get up for real, get dressed, and go to work without her head on straight.

She padded over to the window. Last night's rain had left glittering droplets on the tall, fashionably leafed birch tree. And the birdbaths that had been filled by the downpour shimmered with happiness. All in all, the colors of summer had returned, and the birds were already singing their praises.

She pulled out her yoga mat and saluted the sun that hadn't as yet fully arrived, and then went through a few rudimentary poses to loosen her joints and stretch out the kinks. The exercises were paying off, but now she had to think about course-correcting her diet to make up for the extra portions last night. Being able to see her waist again made the idea of a protein shake for both breakfast and lunch today a whole lot easier to swallow.

Best of all, Ross was expected to call tonight to finalize their plans for Saturday. She had to applaud his plan given their present locales and the logistics that would be required in order to see each other occasionally. She wondered what might happen if those occasions turned into regular schedules. And just as suddenly, she put that idea out of her head.

On the other hand, a day trip—being away from all things familiar, unlocking their inner personality, foibles and all—on neutral ground seemed perfect for a first date. It was what might follow when they made it back home that worried her.

Walking into the kitchen, she spotted the backpack Maggie had propped against the wall the night before. Kate had found her favorite pair of trekkers in the back of her closet last night and placed them next to the backpack and as she looked out the window, she said "When had life become so unpredictable?" The crow bobbed his head, which could if she chose, mean that he was contemplating an answer. And then he flew off to rob another household of its scraps. And she waved at him for good measure.

"The forecast is all blue skies and soft seas," Ross said that evening.

"How poetic," Kate responded. Too bad he couldn't see the way her face glowed in anticipation.

"I'm a poetic kinda guy."

"If you say so; see you in the morning, then."

Kate hung up the phone before she could yammer on. She had been on her own for so long that it was commonplace for her to not only talk to herself, but to search for answers that would fit the topic. Not a good way to impress a new man in her life for sure.

She opened the back door and he'd been right; tomorrow would be a perfect day for a very special boat ride. Then, she filled the small backpack with the 'just in case' items that might not be readily available out on that big rock. By the time she finished, her bedroom was a chaotic mess, and it wasn't as if she hadn't grown up on the water, but this was very different from putting on bright bibbed oil skins, warm shirts, and huge work gloves. For a time, her father had fished in the icy waters off Monhegan, and so she was familiar with the topography, and of course, she'd read and heard enough stories about the art colonies that had been started there in the late nineteenth century. It was obvious the moment one saw the landscape that the island was a 'no car' zone with only small trucks in sight that were only capable of hauling supplies up the hill to their destination.

But this day trip with Ross would have nothing to do with any of that, though it might push her toward taking the painting workshop she'd foregone for the sake of her father's needs. The *Mary-Kate* came first in those days. And by now, those teachers would have grown old, but there would always be someone to inspire, of that, she was sure. So, this would be her very first time to actually set foot on Monhegan Island, and she would be taking those steps with a man who just *might* prove to be a keeper. She looked at her figure in the new full-length mirror, and said, "Don't get your hopes up."

The next morning the sun arrived along with those hopes because she had nothing to lose. It was going to be a glorious day for a boat ride; the *Balmy Days* was meant to take the chop if that were to happen, but she didn't care. She wanted to sit up top, her face to the sun, to breathe in the freedom of the wind as she'd done most of her young life.

In the meantime, she downed a small coffee and a protein shake and slathered up in sunscreen, which had been sorely neglected in her youth. She heard the chirping birds reminding her to fill their baths and then she watered a few of the potted plants, killing time as she waited for Ross.

The horn blew first and then the front end of a black car as sleek as a panther appeared followed by the side panel as Ross rounded the corner. He stopped and hopped out from behind the wheel, his body agile and energetic even when standing still. He grabbed her backpack from her hand and leaned in for a hug. She hugged him back and then he planted a lovely warm kiss on her cheek. "Hi you."

"Hi yourself; that's quite an automobile."

"My chariot awaits," he said as he walked around and opened her door.

"Comfy too," she said as she patted the leather upholstery. "Lots smoother than the warn seats on my dad's old Subaru."

"It gets you where you want to go and that's all that matters," he said. "I traded in a big SUV for this baby when I snagged the job in Boston, and I'm not sorry."

"Me neither," she said as she nestled lower into her seat.

"It suits you."

"So, what are you waiting for…step on it!"

Ross shifted out of her driveway and took a tight turn, and they were off. "Sounds good, right?"

"Sounds great!" Kate turned to look at him, and saw his lips curve upward and waited for him to say something. But he remained in silent concentration until they reached Brunswick. "You look like a boy at Christmas."

"I feel like one. You, this car, a gorgeous day for a boat ride…it's actually better than Christmas, it's like winning the lottery."

"I think you could take me out of the equation, and you'd still be the kid in the candy store just because you're back *home*."

"Have you always been so intuitive?"

"Maybe, I don't know, but I hope I'm right," Kate said. "Everyone should have days like this, and I'm glad I'm part of it."

"Me too," Ross said as he put his hand over hers. "This really was the best idea I've had in a long time."

They remained quiet for the rest of the ride until they reached Boothbay Harbor, and she began to familiarize herself with the shops and restaurants she hadn't seen in years. "Look, the parking lot's almost full."

"The summer people have landed," Ross said. "But we can fit in right over there."

Kate followed his finger as he maneuvered toward into a spot to the left of the *Balmy Days* sign. A few of the day-trippers turned and smiled when they spotted the car.

"I might like to do that one day," Kate said as she pointed to a man standing next to a portable easel and canvas tote."

"I brought my camera along; maybe I can help to inspire you."

"I think we'd better make a run for the boat, first, don't you," Kate said as she hopped out of the car.

"Let's do it," Ross said grabbing their packs.

 "It's been forever since I was out on the water and I didn't realize how much I missed it."

"Well, at least you don't have to earn your keep today, though I promise to give you a good workout on the trails."

"Just be gentle, I haven't hiked in a long time either."

"Don't go soft on me now, girl; we need to work up an appetite for some good brewery beer and pub food to hold us over till I can take you to dinner tonight."

Kate thought of all those calories she'd avoided for weeks and then decided she was being foolish. He wouldn't have asked her out if he'd found her figure faulting or her personality dull. Maggie had been right to suggest that she drop all this nonsense and just be herself. Of course, Maggie had *the* perfect figure, but still thought Kate, it was wrong for her to dwell. She was healthy and that should be enough. "I'll give it the old college try."

"Hop on," Ross said as he reached for her hand.

"I'm all for sitting on the upper deck; that okay with you?"

"I was hoping you'd want to, and look at that sky!"

"Bluebird," she said as the boat pulled away from the pier. "The ideal color for today."

"Are you warm enough," Ross said.

"So far, yes."

They watched the captain maneuver the boat away from the pier and wondered how he would manage to get through all the anchored boats. But she'd forgotten how loud a boat horn could be, and then she spotted a few people waving from the deck of a nearby restaurant. Thankfully, the smell of diesel was taken away by the same breeze that pushed the scent of bacon and maybe cinnamon toast, toward them.

"You look so at home," Ross said.

"I feel at home, and I think this was the best idea you could have come up with."

"I'm a lot smarter than I look."

"Awe, fishing for compliments, are we?"

"Maybe."

"Let's see how the rest of the day goes."

"You are tough!"

She winked at him and they sat comfortably wrapped in their own little worlds and then about an hour in, the wind blew up and the sea turned choppy. Ross put his arm around her, and she accepted it as part of understanding who he might be in a pinch. A small gesture and she was getting cold.

"You're shaking," he said.

"I probably should have expected this to happen, but honestly, I couldn't find my windbreaker," she said. "But we only have another half hour to go."

"Doesn't matter, take mine; I have a heavy sweater underneath."

"If you're sure," she said as her hair was whipped across her face.

"Put this on," he said as he removed his jacket. "Unless you'd rather go below."

The warmth of his body was wrapped in his jacket and she already smelled his aftershave against the smell of the sea. Intoxicating, she thought as she wriggled into the sleeves. "No, this'll be fine, thank you."

"Looks good on you too."

"You mean you like your women in men's clothing."

"You do have a way of twisting my words, don't you?"

"Sorry, I think I'm just a bit gun-shy about men in general these days," Kate said. "But I promise this will be a fun day."

"That's better, and look, there it is," Ross said. "Look at that all those dogs waiting to greet us."

Sure enough, there were five dogs lined up, which upon closer inspection, were all tethered to leashes that were being held by a stoutish woman with gray hair who was waving frantically at a couple who were practically falling overboard waving back. "Their owners look as happy as the pups," Kate said.

The ferry nudged up to the dock and the dogs immediately began to bark and howl, and pulling on their leads, barely able to be contained. "That's the way we should all be greeted," Ross said. "If I didn't work such strange hours, I would love one like that golden on the right."

"I'm kind of partial to the chocolate lab myself," Kate said. "But like you, it's hard to have a pet when they have to be left alone so much."

Finally, cases were unloaded, and the crowd dispersed up the hill toward the Inn and other establishments. She hadn't realized that there were more artists below and now they converged onto the island where they were met by a man driving a small rusted-out truck. Kate watched as they all jumped into the truck bed and were hauled away like the rest of the luggage. A sense of disappointment came over her, a missed opportunity perhaps, but one that she had the chance to make right in the near future if she really wanted to. But then, she looked at Ross and that feeling completely dissipated. "Where do we go from here?"

"Upward and onward!" Ross said.

"Here, take this," Kate said returning his jacket. "I'll do better without it and I'm warm enough on land."

"Let's head toward the lighthouse, then, and go from there."

They walked quickly at first, and then Kate sensed she really was out of shape and he slowed to match her pace. It was still a good workout and she made a silent promise to go back to the gym. And then, they came to the clearing that looked out over Black Head cliff, the location that had launched a thousand paintings. As had most of the spots on this rocky outpost. And by the time they got back to the village, Ross had taken more than enough photos and promised to send them to her in case she had caught the painting bug again.

They grabbed a quick sandwich to go and continued on until they came upon the last remains of the D.T. Sheridan. Ross examined the rusty metal and they then circled back to Fish Beach where a few of the painters from the boat had taken up their positions. Gulls circled overhead. "The light has changed many times since they started," Kate said.

"Difficult to paint?" Ross asked.

"Very, which is why I'd always thought I'd be a studio painter, but then I stopped altogether."

"I'm sorry there wasn't time for Cathedral Wood," Ross said as they reached a bench. "Maybe next time?"

"Are you asking me out on another date?"

"You know damn well I am," he said as he leaned in to kiss her.

It was a simple buss on the cheek, but she turned her head without thinking and his lips landed on hers. "Oh!"

"No, wow!" Ross said.

She stared at him, her body warming and her face heating up; she wasn't certain if it was another flush or just the reaction to his kiss, but it didn't matter. "That *was* nice."

"Nice, my foot, it was great!" Ross said as he leaned in for another.

"How about we make our way back to the dock so we don't miss our ride?"

"As I said before, you are tough."

"Just cautious," Kate said as she grabbed his hand and pulled him to his feet.

"You win, but I won't stop trying."

"I had a feeling you wouldn't and maybe I won't mind; we'll see."

They walked hand in hand and joined the line of people readying to board along with more boxes and crates, but this time without the artists. "Looks like the painters are in for a few beautiful days at their easels," Kate said.

"You sound like you'd rather stay than leave."

"Not this time, but we'll see."

"Wanta sit below for the ride home?"

"Not really, but we probably should; the wind has kicked up and my face is already sunburned."

They found a seat in the large cabin, but Ross squeezed as close as possible to keep her warm.

"Tell me about your grandparents," Kate said.

"Daniel and Helen Anderson…two of the most generous people you'd ever meet."

"Anderson," Kate said. "I wonder if my dad knows the family."

"Gramps was a retired lineman by the time they moved to Hull Island, and Gran was, well what can I say, a spitfire, taking charge of the polls on election day, rounding up the kids for Halloween parties at the cottage, and doing almost anything to please me."

"Sounds wonderful."

"Do I detect a note of sadness."

"Maybe, I don't know," Kate said. "Mine weren't present that's all, and more than anything, I wish I'd known my grandmother Brigid."

"What about your grandfather?"

"In a nutshell, James Flannagan was a sea captain who died at sea and left more than one mystery behind," Kate said. "And being out on Monhegan today made me think of Gran all over again; sometimes I wonder if she met her fate there or if she just ran away to get away from him."

"That's a cliffhanger, you have to tell me the story."

"Not now, but maybe over dinner, which I think will be an early one. All that sun and wind has made me very hungry."

They rode the rest of the way in silence, giving in to the loud hum of the engines and chatter of those seated nearby. "Wake up sleepy head," Ross said into Kate's ear.

"I didn't think I was that tired," Kate said. "But I haven't had that much outdoor exercise in a very long time."

"I hope you're still hungry."

"It seems that I never lose my appetite," Kate chuckled. "But how about we head right to Brunswick and eat there and then we can have coffee at my place before you have to drive home."

"I like that idea a whole lot."

Kate had no idea they would end up at the Inn and of course, the waiter and bartender recognized her, which gave Ross a laughing fit. "You never mentioned how popular you are."

"Not, just memorable…it's the hair I think."

"Bullpucky," Ross said with a big grin. "You have no idea how exotically beautiful you are, do you?"

"No one has ever called me exotic, though I have heard the word beautiful on occasion," she teased.

"I told you before you could have been the subject of a painting, but then again, you never believe a word I say."

"Don't pout, please, it will ruin my day, and see that waiter over there watching us," Kate said. "He will come over here and berate me because as far as he's concerned, you are way more gorgeous. Trust me, I found that out the hard way."

"That last guy you went out with?"

"Uh huh."

"I'm starving, what do you recommend?"

"The burger or maybe the big salad, which is what I think I'm going to have."

"Don't be silly; let's have a good old-fashioned porterhouse…with all the trimmings."

"If you say so, and I'll have a big glass of water with a red wine chaser," Kate said to the waiter who had sidled into their space.

"How've you been, Kate?"

"Just fine, George; meet my friend Ross."

"And what would you like to drink, Ross?"

"Why don't you bring us a bottle of this red," Ross said pointing to the name on the drinks menu.

"Coming right up—great choice."

"You've made his day," Kate said as she watched George look back over his shoulder.

"He's a nice fellow."

"Just don't lead him on please."

"That would be plain cruel; I'm not like that, Kate, truly."

"I'm just kidding, honest; I think you are very kind," Kate said. "Look how well you looked after me today."

"I think I'd like to look after you a little more if you don't mind," Ross said just as he leaned in to kiss her.

"This is getting to be a habit."

"And a very good one indeed."

"Ahem!"

"Sorry, George, we'll behave."

"Here, let me take this," Ross said as he reached for the bottle and began to pour the wine into Kate's glass.

"Do you want to place your dinner order now?"

"Absolutely, George, we're starving!" Ross smiled at Kate and said, "How do you like your steak?"

She looked at George and said, "Medium rare, please."

"Mine too, George."

"Be up in a little bit," George said as he left them staring into each other's eyes.

Chapter 36

"So, this is what you do when you're in Maine," Ross said.

"I *dabble* in color, and I'm so glad that I do; this place was nice enough but it lacked personality, so I tried to put my spin on it and my landlord, who's a bit of a snob about decorating, actually agreed to let me have my way."

"How could he not," Ross said as he draped his arm over her shoulder. "What's the rest of the place look like?"

"Let me put the coffee on and I'll show you," Kate said as she scooped out from beneath his arm and hurried over to the counter.

"You seem a little skittish; please know that I wouldn't do anything to push you away."

"I know; it's just new, that's all."

"Then, let's take it slow; coffee and a little conversation and I'll go home, promise."

"Take a look around while I get out the cups," Kate said. "Milk and sugar?"

"Black, thanks," Ross said as he headed toward the living room. "Oh, this is really nice, Kate, and I do love this leather chair."

"Old man Flannagan's prize possession, or so I've been told," Kate shouted.

"Read much?"

"Don't be snide," she said as she walked in with a small tray. "I adore books."

"Here let me take this," Ross said as he reached for the tray. "Where do you want me to put it?"

"Right there's fine," Kate said as she hurried to clear a small mound of books from the cocktail table.

"Have you read all of these?"

"Most of them, but I'm in the process of culling them out, that's why they are all over the place, so that I can make sure I'm finished with them."

"I simply don't have time to read as often as I'd like," Ross said as he picked up his coffee.

"I'd be happy to give you any one of them if you'd like; maybe that one over there...the one on Renaissance paint colors."

"So, you were listening to me."

"Of course," Kate said. "Did you think I'd forget anyone who had fallen in love with that gallery the way you had."

"Maybe we should talk more about love at another time," Ross said. "I'm afraid I'll overstep my welcome and it's getting late."

"Thank you for a very special day," Kate said as she went up on her toes to kiss him goodnight.

"Here, let me do this the right way," Ross said as he pulled her to him.

Kate started to say something and then he planted a kiss that nearly took her breath away. "I've been wanting to do that all day," he said as he stood back a few inches. "And now that I have, I'd like permission to do it again."

"Permission granted," Kate said as she took the first step forward.

By the time she walked him to the door, they'd spent twenty minutes saying goodnight in the living room, having moved to the couch where he could run his fingers through her hair and over the skin of her neck, kiss her ears and her eyelids, cup her breasts, only to have her wanting more. "I didn't expect that," she said as she stood with her hand on the doorknob.

"A little too soon?"

"Maybe, maybe not; depends on whether we enjoyed it as much as I think we did."

"Maybe more than we thought we would?"

"Maybe we should get to know each other a little better before we decide?"

"How about I come back up next weekend?"

"How about you do that; I'm sure I can find some time for you."

"See, you are tough, but beautiful," Ross said as he leaned in for one last kiss.

"Go now, before I change my mind!"

"Going, but I'll call you tomorrow before I leave for Boston."

And then he was gone. Kate could see him in the glow of the porch light, the way his body slid into the driver's seat, the tilt of his head as he blew her a kiss, the shadow of the sleek car leaving her property. "It's going to be a very long week," she whispered into the cool air.

Chapter 37

"So how was it?" Maggie asked just as Kate picked up the phone.

"You couldn't wait until I'd brushed my teeth and had my coffee?"

"It's your day off, I thought you'd be in bed reading and wouldn't mind giving me the scoop about your date."

"That's exactly right…it's Sunday and I wish it were next weekend already; oh my God, he is amazing!"

"Poor me a cup, I'm on my way over!"

"I'll put on a fresh pot; the cup that's left is from last night."

Ten minutes later, Maggie rushed in through the mud room door and said, "I brought donuts and don't say a word about calories. These were left over from Paul's visit and I can't eat them all by myself."

"Cinnamon swirls?" Kate said. "No, I'd prefer that chocolate sprinkled one and you'd better not tell me that was yours."

"Anything you want, just spill the beans."

"We walked all over Monhegan and…"

"Let me stop you right there; what happened later?"

"We ended up at the Inn at Brunswick Station, where Paul and I had our first date, and believe it or not the waiter recognized me and then he made eyes at Ross, just like he had with Paul, and…"

"Skip ahead, please!"

"Oh, all right; we came back here for coffee and we talked and talked and then he started kissing me, and don't get all googly-eyed, nothing happened, at least not what you're thinking, but we started acting like a couple of teens, you know, necking as if you're in the back seat of his father's car and you realize you've gone just a tad too far and you have to extricate yourself and rearrange your clothes."

"Take a breath, I get the picture," Maggie said. "You actually do sound like a teen, but was it enjoyable, you know, being your first time and all that?"

"Now you're making fun of me, but yes it was beyond enjoyable; it was everything I'd hoped from the moment I laid eyes on him but couldn't possibly vocalize for fear of ruining the idea. It was moonbeams and roses, and all the rest."

"Now I know you're not well," Maggie said.

"I'm more than well, I'm back!" Kate said. "My skin tingled and my body flushed all my anxieties away and I felt like I was coming back to life after a long winter siege."

"You do have a flair for the dramatic."

"I don't care; it's mostly your fault anyway; you're the one who's been going on and on about my getting back into the game."

"And I've created someone I've never known."

"Yes, you have so you better get used to this new version, because unless I'm totally off the mark, Ross will be making a few weekend pilgrimages to Hull Island."

"All kidding aside," Maggie said. "Let me just hug you for being so brave and stepping outside your comfort zone; you're beaming."

"Can we eat the donuts now?"

An hour and a half later and two more cups of coffee, Kate opened the door and watched Maggie walk to her car. "Do I still have to go out with that guy you found," she yelled.

"Not unless you want to."

"I think I'll pass if you don't mind," Kate said as Maggie began to walk back toward her.

"Just think it over for another day or so, just in case it would be good to have options," Maggie said. "Do that for me, okay?"

"If you put it that way, okay, but it'll have to be a weeknight and not at the Inn for dinner; George wouldn't be able to handle it."

"Don't worry about George, think about yourself and how this could all be an illusion; after all, you are on the rebound."

"Thanks for reminding me," Kate said. "I'm smart enough to know you're right, but I wish you could have felt the way his lips felt…"

"Here we go again; I'm leaving now."

Kate winked at her and watched her head down the walk to her car and into the warm air and let out a sigh. It was good to be loved by a friend, and it was wonderful to anticipate the love of a good man. She only hoped he really was, but she would wait and voice that the next time she talked with Maggie. No point in spoiling the morning.

Chapter 38

As soon as Ross hung up the phone, Kate headed out to Thornton Oaks to have Sunday lunch with her father. It was spur of the moment, but her mood was such that she couldn't bear the idea of staying in and reading all day, which is something she might normally do on Sunday. And the weather was glorious, good enough to take her dad out for a spin if he was up to it.

Unfortunately, he wasn't as she found out the moment that she walked into the dining hall. His day nurse, Trudy, was trying to calm him down and he looked up and saw Kate and started flailing his arms.

Kate rushed over and helped him stand while Trudy cleared away his plate. They'd been seated away from the center of the room in front of a favorite window. "What on earth happened," Kate asked.

"One of the groundskeepers walking along the path," Trudy said. "I don't exactly know why, but he waved his cap and your dad immediately changed. "I'm so sorry, I know how much you wanted to sit and eat a meal together."

"Let me walk you upstairs," Kate said. "You come too, Trudy, maybe some light will be shed that will be helpful later."

Tom Flannagan looked from one to the other and said, "When do we get dessert?"

"I brought some chocolate, Dad, for you and Trudy to share."

"Good, let's go to my room, then."

"Sure sounds like a plan," Kate said as she winked at Trudy. "This isn't exactly what I had in mind, but I'll make sure he's settled before I leave."

And they managed to do just fine, sharing the candy, watching a little TV together and finally, Trudy got the point across to Kate's father that it was time for a nap and once again, Kate watched, a little jealous if she was being honest, at how easily his nurse was able to get him into his bedroom.

As soon as Trudy came out, Kate went in and kissed him and told him that she'd be back soon.

"He seems peaceful enough," she said to Trudy as she walked back into the living room.

"He's fine for now, but I can't promise this won't happen again."

"I know, but I can't keep hoping that something will change even though I know that it probably won't."

"Go and have a lovely rest of the day, Kate; I'll call you if I need you."

Kate drove all the way to Cove's End before the tears escaped. Why was life so cruel, why did he have to be the one this happened to. Hadn't his life been hard enough, she thought as she sat in the car and cried her eyes out.

Chapter 39

June slipped into July before Kate would admit that she had fallen hard. She even brought him by to meet her dad, which went surprisingly well and she credited Ross for handling the situation with such aplomb.

And then Ross frequented Maine with more urgency; they began to spend their weekends together at her cottage on Hull Island. When he couldn't be in Maine, she took the train to Boston. And their friendship grew. Better still, the sex was amazing; she'd almost forgotten the joys of bedding Angus Larabee, and when she remembered, she made sure not to compare. After all, they were now mature adults and nothing would ever be as it was in their twenties.

"So, what are you doing on the fourth?" Maggie asked as they finished their drinks out on the deck of her cottage.

"Going down to Boston, I think, why?"

"Jim and I are putting on a feast and I thought maybe you and Ross would like to join us."

"How's that working out for you," Kate asked. "You've been seeing him, what, three and a half weeks, now."

"Four and a half, but who's counting," Maggie said. "But it is working out; I like him and he's just young enough to be fun without making me look foolish."

"You could never look foolish; no one can tell how old you are either. I, on the other hand, have all the markings of a fifty-year-old, right down to things that are beginning to sag with every pound I lose."

"You just need a little more exercise and I don't mean the kind that you seem to be receiving these days."

"I don't know what you're talking about," Kate said with a gleam in her eye. "I promise we'll get together with you guys the next time; *there will always be a next time, right?*"

"You have the memory of an elephant!"

"I'm just happy that it's true," Kate said as Maggie walked her to the door.

The Downeaster has become the playland of her imagination these past weeks, a place to contemplate the latest chapters in her life. She loved going back to Boston for events like those on the fourth of July, but she loved coming home to Hull Island even more. All the doubt about Ross that she'd held tight in the beginning had melted away now that she had indeed fallen hard, harder than she thought possible, hard enough to regret leaving him for the morning train. That's when he'd made inroads toward her staying: permanently.

"Not gonna happen," she whispered to her reflection in the window as the train passed the now familiar towns and communities. She'd given up on the novel she'd brought along, but she couldn't resist closing her eyes, could not allow the image of Ross in his workout clothes to fall away…his muscular body, the naughty grin on his face, his welcoming arms the moment she had arrived in the city. Had that only been two days ago, she thought as she recognized the deepening power of love. Theirs had turned into a whirlwind romance; wining and dining and impressive weekend jaunts. Declarations of love shouted from the top of Cadillac Mountain and from the edges of the sea as they wandered Monhegan Island for a second time.

She understood that he wasn't happy with her decision, but she'd vowed not to cave in to any man ever again; besides, each time she returned to the city, she thought of her own cottage with a newfound respect. Ross's one-bedroom apartment was glistening with stainless steel and hard edges and squeaky-clean granite surfaces; obviously not used for entertaining or even eating at home, not unless he had a maid, which she quickly found out, he didn't.

Ross had promised that he would try and work something out so that they could be together on a more regular basis; he also wanted her to stay at his Hull Island cottage the next time he returned to Maine.

For all this time, she'd shrugged off the idea, saying that it was just easier to be in her own space since he'd obviously not been able to spend enough time there after his grandparents turned it over to him, not enough to make it a home anyway. More like a hotel, which then meant they'd have to stock in food even though she already had enough for them both. What she hadn't said and more to the point, unlike the city apartment, his island house needed a real overhauling. It was dank, musty and out of date and she didn't want to be the one to clean it or redo it unless she was going to move in and that didn't seem like it would happen anytime soon.

The train slowed and this time when she stepped off the Downeaster at Brunswick Station, she had no desire to stay at the Inn for the night, no thought of trying to unwind with a martini and a hot bath. She was totally sated and glowing and realized that it wouldn't matter what she ate or drank or where she stayed, with the exception of wherever Ross happened to be. Sadly, she hadn't been able to voice her qualms about his grandparents' house, but maybe she would now that he was contemplating a move to Maine.

Chapter 40

"Guess what?" Ross said.

"What," Kate said.

"I've found someone I can delegate to run the Boston end of my business, which means that I can set up the management end from my cottage on Hull Island. Which means that you might consider moving in with me; mind you I said, might."

Kate had only been in the kitchen of Ross's old Victorian, at least that's the type of construction she thought the house would be classified as. Lots of fretwork on the outside, but she hadn't been further inside than the kitchen and it was in definite need of a remodel. "It's a charming looking house, but I'm not sure I'm ready for a complete uprooting from the simplicity of this cottage," Kate said.

"I know you think the house is too big, and in a way, it is, but I could have things changed any way you'd like: upgraded appliances, screened in porch…I know you'd love a swing."

"Oh, that's unfair; just because I went a little overboard about that when we were Down East in Castine, but that doesn't mean I expect you to have one installed just for me."

"I'd do it if it would make you happy."

"Tell you what; next time I'll make dinner for you at *your* house instead of mine and we'll talk about it then—okay?"

"More than okay; but it won't be until next month since I now have to pull out all the stops in order to get Jorge on board to take my place in the city."

"So, how's everything going with Ross?" Maggie asked.

"I can't believe how good it is; you know how skeptical I've been."

"I also know that you really do glow and that can only be from the way you feel; am I right?"

"You are one hundred percent right, and I can't thank you enough for encouraging me to take a chance on love again."

"So, when do you move in with him, or he with you for that matter?"

"That's the only sticky wicket," Kate said. "I'm not sure I want us to *live* together; not yet anyway. His place has been rented out for a long time and even though I haven't had a total tour, the kitchen and downstairs powder room are really outdated and frankly, musty as hell. It's like the previous tenants never bothered to pick up a dust rag.

"And as to my place...well, that's it, it is *my* place unless the landlord tosses me out. And I forgot to mention that he's offered me the opportunity to buy from him now that I've made it into such a nice home, which means I'm not sure that I do want to share it."

"Well now, haven't we come a long way since those days of crying your eyes out for Angus, and aren't I one grateful friend," Maggie said.

"It's me who's grateful; without you I might still be sitting in a puddle of tears in my kitchen, which if you remember was painted plain old white at the time."

"How about you and I taking a day trip to the Farnsworth this coming weekend since Ross will be in Boston doing what he needs to do."

"I think that would be perfect, and putting a little distance between us might just be the right move at the right time."

"God, you're getting smart," Maggie said as she started to pat herself on the back.

"Take credit all you want, but it's true, without you I'd still be sitting on the kitchen floor wondering what my life would be like ten years from now."

"Speaking of now, how about we run into Brunswick for a bite to eat."

"I hope you're driving," Kate said. "My eyes are beginning to cross from too much reading."

"Sure; you drove the last time anyway…pick you up in an hour."

"What's happening with your gran's diary; did you find the missing pages?" Maggie said.

"I'm embarrassed that I stopped searching…because of Ross and going back and forth to Boston."

"You won't give up though, right?"

"Of course not; I just don't know where else to look, and my visits with Dad are not what I'd hoped either," Kate said. "He's spiraling and I even brought Ross to meet him the last time he was here, which I thought would cheer him up, but he just went silent on us."

"That's so sad."

"It really is, and no matter how much I wish it away, he's never going to be himself again, so I've decided to record some of my fondest memories before life takes over and I forget them too."

"What a great idea," Maggie said as she pulled into a parking spot. "Let's get inside where you can tell me all about it."

"Pizza, the perfect meal for someone eating low-carb this week."

"Not again; I swear I can't keep track, but you can have a salad if you want."

"Just kidding; he's been doing such a good job keeping me in shape that I think I can splurge a little."

"Don't gloat," Maggie said. "It's not becoming."

Chapter 41

Kate and Maggie shared more than one dinner during Ross's stint in Boston. And her workdays remained the same with the exception of one new client, a Mrs. Broadmoor who was recently widowed and truly only needed to be listened to. Kate considered how lonely she had been after her divorce and started bringing Mrs. B (as she liked to be called now) the occasional takeout meal from one of Kate's favorite restaurants: the Nobel Tavern.

In the evenings, she spent as much time with Maggie as she could; they'd developed a penchant for scrabble and monopoly. And tonight, Paul was joining them as he often did when in the area.

"No cheating ladies," Paul said as he stepped into his sister's kitchen.

"Look what the cat dragged in, Kate."

"He does look familiar," Kate said. "How's your hunt for the perfect woman coming along?"

"From what I've heard, not nearly as well as what you've got going."

"Maggeeee!"

"Yes, Kate, I told him you were head over heels; what'd you expect."

"A little discretion maybe, but wait, you don't do discretion, right Paul?"

"Oh, it's gang up on Mags tonight, is it; well just so you know, I'm winning the pot and you guys aren't getting any sympathy."

"What else is new!" Paul exclaimed as he helped himself to a glass of wine and took a seat at the table.

The night wore on until they'd exhausted all the properties on the board and were into telling stories. "I have to go home or I won't be able to drive," Paul said.

"You can bunk here if you want, but then you'd have to put up with the cat; did I tell you I have a cat?"

"You do not; you know I'm allergic," said Paul.

"Oh god, don't you two ever quit!" Kate said as she began to clear the table.

"I'm gone," Paul said. "Thank you both for a most enlightening evening."

"I'm outta here too," Kate said.

"Fleeing the sinking ship?" said Maggie

"Fleeing the cat!" said Paul

"You do know she's kidding, right," said Kate as they walked to their cars.

"Of course, but she's happier when I play along."

And so it went; days and nights of friendship-building and then it was time for Ross to return. As they'd agreed, Kate would cook dinner at his place and now as she packed up the food, she remembered to put a few things in her tote just in case she decided to stay over. And of course, that depended on whether or not the bedroom was in better condition than the kitchen.

Kate had worn leggings and a long sweater and ballet flats for her first dinner in Ross's house. It was one of those late summer evenings; the air was filled with the scent of roses that had been planted long before either of them had been born. The porch lights were on and the light from the living room filtered out through the front window. Smoke from the fireplace drifted down around her as she walked up to meet him. Dressed in a soft yellow sweater with tan slacks he was collegiate and sexy at the same time. His hair was shorter than she remembered, but it suited him well.

"Let me take these," Ross said as he grabbed the bag of food while simultaneously kissing her squarely on the forehead.

"What a night, look at that sky."

"There's the milky way," Ross said as he turned her around and pointed upward.

"I thought that was Orion's Belt."

"No, that's over there."

Kate turned him back around and said, "If you want to eat, we'd better get these groceries inside so I can get started."

"I have a nice wine breathing on the kitchen table."

"Does that really make a different; it seems like it all tastes the same once it's poured."

"Not according to the chefs that I work with, but that's a whole other conversation," Ross said as he steered her into the kitchen. "Tonight, is about us."

Kate pulled out a drawer she hoped contained the knives and then one that she remembered as the place for pots and pans. The house had been aired out and Ross had lit a few candles and by the time she had the sauce simmering, the only thing they could smell were Italian seasonings and plenty of garlic. "Good thing we're both eating the same food," she said as she walked over to kiss him. "Otherwise, one of us would have to go home early."

"Good thing I love garlic," Ross said as he wrapped her in his arms. "And while that's simmering away and the water hasn't come to a boil yet, how about I give you the thirty-cent tour of this old house, starting with these back stairs."

"Sounds like a PBS program, but I think you're trying to lure me into one of the unused bedrooms to have your way with me."

"Maybe, maybe not; we'll see," Ross said as he snapped on a single light that exposed a vividly stark stairwell.

"This is a little spooky."

"It leads to what had once been the maid's quarter, before my grands' time and before they turned it into a hobby room with an electric train for me."

"Is it still there?"

"No, I sold it to a collector just before I put the house on the rental market, and now I kinda wish I hadn't done that."

Ross pulled her into a large square-shaped room and she immediately began to sneeze. "I'm sorry; I can't be in here," Kate said. "It's my stupid allergies; I think I have something in my purse that'll help."

"I should have thought of that before I dragged you upstairs; here take my hand so you don't trip."

Once they were back in the kitchen, Kate found an allergy tab in her purse, one of those quick release types that she had to rely on in situations like this. She hadn't been plagued by allergies in the city, but Maine was a different matter. "Grab me a platter for the cheese, please," she asked as she opened a box of Triscuits.

"Any particular size," Ross asked.

"Just big enough for this block of Chedder and a few crackers." Kate said as she searched for a box of salt in the cupboard.

"I only just brought in the staples and never thought to put that on a lower shelf, but then I hardly cook for myself," Ross said as he reached over her head for the salt.

Kate took the salt from his hand and added a palm full into the boiling water and then emptied the box of pasta in after it. "Let me just stir this and then you can show me the rest of the downstairs," she said as she turned off the burner under the saucepan.

"This way to the living room, where as you can see, I've got a nice little fire going and…"

"That's my grandmother!" Kate yelled. "That's my missing painting!"

"Yours, it's mine, and that's my grandmother," Ross said as he pointed to the right side of the painting?"

"But that's Brigid!"

"That's your grandmother; that woman was my grandmother's best friend."

"Who was your grandmother?"

"Helen Budreau before she became Helen Anderson."

"Budreau; is that the B on your business card?"

"Yeh, I'm Ross Budreau Anderson, why?"

"My grandmother's diary; I have what's left of it and there's lots of pages about what was happening with her friend, Helen," Kate said as she looked back and forth between the painting and Ross's expression. What was going on; how could this painting be in his cottage and who actually owned it? "I don't get it; all this time and it's been here—all this time."

"There's only one way we can resolve this," Ross said and he pulled her onto the sofa.

"We can't resolve this with a few glasses of wine and a little romance, not on your life."

"What am I supposed to do; it's been in my grandparents' possession for as long as I can remember and I never knew that woman posing with my gran was your grandmother."

"Did you ever wonder about the artist?"

"Not really; I mean it's a nice painting—quite good actually, but not one of the greats, and you of all people can see that given all the time you've spent at the Gardner."

"But this is personal, and I think it's a remarkable piece, and I think I'm going to explode from wonder and sadness at the same time. To think I've been worried about finding it and now it's right here in front of me.'

"Should we have it appraised?"

"We?"

"Well, it is technically mine."

"Can you prove provenance?"

"Can you?" Ross asked.

Kate suddenly felt the entire evening about to spiral out of control. "Can you take it down, please, I need to see it up close."

"Gran had it reframed a long time ago, and the framer used brown paper as a backing; maybe there's something written there: a date or what you're calling provenance."

"I can't believe you never turned it around?"

"I can't believe how worked up you're getting; it's like I hardly know you," Ross said. "Besides, why would I look at the back of a painting that's been in their possession for years; there'd been no reason for me to do that."

"Maybe, but you have no idea how much this painting means to me, so can you please take it down, now!"

"Look, take a sip of your wine and let me grab a stool so I don't have to try and lift it off the hook and maybe rip the paper."

"It does looks heavy."

"That's why I want the stool," Ross repeated as if she were a child waiting for a Christmas present. And that's exactly how she looked: her eyes wide with anticipation and then he saw that she was close to tears. He pulled her to her feet and hugged her and then he went into the hall closet where the stool had always been stored.

Kate bent down and picked up her glass and walked over to the fireplace and looked up at the woman she'd been longing to meet. Her heart seemed so full and yet so sad; how had this come to be in this house and what was going on with the universe, especially tonight?

"Here we go," Ross said as he came back into the room.

She watched the way his long fingers grasp the stool and the way his back curved as he set the stool down to the right of the fireplace. She had to admit that everything about his movements were an act of reverence and she was struggling to keep it together. She watched as he reached up and placed one hand on the side and the other on the bottom of the frame in order to heft the weight of the painting up off the hook and then hand it down to her.

"Careful," he said as she reached up to meet the bottom edge of the frame. "It might not be large, but it's really heavy."

"Here all this time, I thought I was just spinning my wheels and there wasn't a painting to be found and now, this," she said as she caught the frame solidly between her hands. "Now what?"

"Take it over to that lamp, and we'll see if there's anything written on the back," Ross said. "The light is much better there and well, I don't know, maybe since it was Gran's chair…"

Kate saw that he was trying, and she felt a lump in her throat; she was being so harsh with him for no reason. "This looks like the type of print that my mother would have loved," she said as she went over to a large wing chair with a floor lamp behind it.

The lamp was also a familiar style, one that Kate remembered from childhood: seated on her mother's lap with the glow of peach-colored silk radiating from a bell-shaped lampshade. "Get over here," she said before he could remove the stool. "I need to hug you first."

He watched as she set the painting up against the chair as gently as if she were handling a small child. And he walked over to her open arms. "We'll get through this together, okay?"

"Let's get this over with, then," she said as she turned the painting around and propped it on the chair arms while she carefully patted down the paper backing.

"I don't see any writing," Ross said as he followed her hand.

"Me either, but wait, I feel something," she said as she smoothed her hand back and forth on the lower right corner, where perhaps whatever it was had fallen downward when it was hung.

"Hang on, let me get a knife or some scissors so we can slit the paper; I don't want to tear off the entire backing unnecessarily."

"Maybe I should just rip it off in lieu of all this fuss and bother about the damn backing."

"You're getting awfully hot under the collar; I'm not the enemy here, Kate."

"Please just get scissors or something or I swear I will rip it."

"There's a pair in the kitchen; hang on."

Kate had all she could do not to tear the backing off in one fell swoop, but he was right, she was getting way too angry; this was not his fault. "I'm sorry," she said the moment he walked back into the room.

"I'm sorry too; let's just see what we have here first; remember, I love you."

"I know, it's just that you can't imagine what reading Gran's diary did to me; my grandfather was such a bastard."

"Then, here, take the scissors and cut a nice neat slice around whatever you think is there."

Kate kissed him, hard, and before he could respond, she turned away and put her left hand over what felt like a soft bulge, and then with her right hand, she gently cut around whatever was there letting the sharp tip of the scissors do all the work, the way she would when she cut through wrapping paper; just a simple slide and then there it was, an envelope intended for a greeting card of some sort, and it was addressed to Tommy Flannagan.

Ross slipped his finger under the flap and it fell open easily. A letter-sized paper had been folded over, which had caused the bulging, and he said, "It's for your father!"

Kate's eyes began to overflow with tears, but she took the proffered letter. She swiped her eyes with her sleeve and then, she began to read Helen Budreau's words:

Well, I guess you'd be Thomas by now and maybe married with children and I know you'd be a successful fisherman, it was in your genes, at least being at sea was. There's so much to say but I'm afraid it won't be easy to hear, so I'll be as helpful as I can and as gentle as I know how...not one of my strong suits as you may remember.

When your Mum disappeared, I knew in my heart it was your father's fault; James was as mean as they came. But he did love you, at least the best way he knew how to, which might not have seemed like much to a small boy. The reason for this letter and the painting is that I had promised your mum—my dear friend and confidante—that I would hide it and protect it from being destroyed. It was the only thing of beauty she ever had beside you, Tommy boy. Do you remember how I used to call you that, you and your sweet curiosity; the months you stayed with me when your Dad was out to sea and how we kept saying Mum was always coming back. She loved you beyond measure, so I know she would have if she could have.

At first I thought she'd just stayed out on Monhegan with the artist who painted this painting but he came back and thought she was here on Hull Island. That's when I suspected that your father may have taken matters into his own hands; he suspected her of cheating and sadly, he would have been right. But hers was no ordinary matter; she loved that Canelli almost as much as she loved you and she couldn't live with James even if he threatened her and she never would have left you alone if she'd had a choice.

It is my fear that James lured her out to the Lady Dora and that he pushed her overboard, though no one could prove it since he never reported her missing. Just kept to himself and when asked said she was over visiting family and so on. Just went about his work and caring however he could for you, and then of course, he went down with the ship in that bad storm, so maybe there's some retribution to be found in that. I believed he was evil, but it was my duty to care for you no matter what—I'd sworn it to your Mum when she told me she was going to visit Canelli out there on Monhegan, but just for a few days. I'll never know for sure what happened, and Tommy I'm so so sorry I couldn't protect her better.

I hope now that you're a grown man, that you can find it in your heart to forgive me; I did the best that I could and then, your Da took you home from my house and swore he'd turn you into a righteous man and a first-class seaman. You loved the ocean, but I knew from the start you loved the fishing boats better than the schooners, so I imagine you have one by now.

God bless you son, and may you have a wonderful life and promise me, that you'll say a prayer for Brigid's soul too. I do every single night of my life.

With love,

Auntie Helen

p.s. If you are reading this then you know what all the fuss and scandal was about. She was a beautiful woman who needed to be seen and never was.

Kate's face twisted into an expression she wouldn't have recognized had there been a mirror. "What did he do!" she screamed. "My poor father; no wonder he behaves so strangely, and it can't all be from Alzheimer's."

"It's the most tragic thing I've ever heard, and think how my Gran must have felt being so responsible," Ross said.

"What are we going to do," Kate said. "How will I make this right?"

"First off, should we bring this to your dad before I leave town again?"

"You don't know how much I want to but I'm worried it might set him off or, oh I don't know what to do."

"For the moment, nothing; you have to be spent and I'm sure the pasta is overcooked by now, so we might be eating eggs, and…"

"Oh, god, I forgot dinner; can you forgive me."

"Nothing to forgive; you've had quite a shock, but how about I hang this back up for now and we can sit here and enjoy our grandmothers and their mutual beauty."

She waited until he'd hung the painting over the mantel and as soon as he sat beside her on the couch, she scooched in close and said, "It's the only way for tonight that I can see us both winning."

"It's not really a contest and there is a tiny solution, well maybe not so tiny, but a reasonable one at least."

"Pray tell," she said as she touched his face, the fine shadow of a beard that he would make disappear in the morning.

"We could get married and the painting would then become joint property: problem solved."

She had thought about this moment ever since they had come home from Monhegan the second time; there'd been something so complete between them that it was still hard to define. "I don't want to battle over this, Ross," she said through tears that were starting afresh, "you're away more than here and I need this painting with me, where it belongs, at least for now."

"Does that mean you're rejecting my proposal?"

Tomorrow, she would go back to her own cottage and contemplate planting azaleas next season; she'd use her gardening bible as a guide so those flowers would blend with the ruthless mix Mother Nature had supplied. And if she could stand it, they would be in orange; she already pictured them dripping with dew and sparkling in the sun. And eventually, she and Ross would compare them to those at the Gardner, because no matter where they lived, they would revisit the museum at every opportunity.

His longing for her was evident, but she had come to realize during these past few years that defeat was not a compatible color, not one that matched her skin, hair, eyes or personality, not any longer. Instead, she put her hand around the back of his neck and pulled him toward her, their longing already building, and she said, "My darling handsome man, thank you, but if you can handle it, I would rather be *your* lover than a wife to anyone. I want us to cook together, share thoughts on books and art, and dance with abandon. And be apart once in a while to recharge—for as long as we deem possible."

Ross stared into her eyes and pulled her up from the sofa and held her close until a piece of paper wouldn't have fit between them. He began a slow dance and quietly hummed the words from "Hallelujah." Kate then stroked his hair and curled her fingers into the fibers of his sweater; and then she sent up a silent thank you to Mr. Cohen for the second time in her life.

Epilogue

The smell of orange, a basket full of them gifted by the staff to celebrate my progress. It's Dr. Benjamin's win of course, but the new meds have allowed me to see more clearly into my windowless world. I have never been a dreamer, but now that I'm waking from the stupor of disease, even if only for a little while each day, I want to believe that I might one day dream of my mother, Brigid. I never told anyone about the letter she left me though it is nearly in tatters from being abused by small fingers that have grown into meatier ones. I only know that without it, I would not have made it through my childhood, not even with Helen's help and caring kindness. To say nothing of harboring me against every storm that my father brought into our house.

I've been sitting on the letter, literally, since Kate's visit earlier this morning. I'd only just found it again, thanks to the new medication. And now that I've seen the painting in person after so many years, I'm doubly comforted by my mother's words:

My dear little man, I don't know if you'll ever forgive me for leaving, but there wasn't any choice at all. It was either do as James said and leave immediately or lose you to the court of public opinion in a case I couldn't refute. I've been branded by names you are too young to understand, but I have loved only one man in my life, and he is Giacomo Canelli. And even he cannot save me from the cruelty your father will inflict if I don't obey him now. I let your auntie Helen think James was about to do something drastic, maybe lose me at sea or something, knowing that she understood my predicament. She loved you as her own anyway, and I knew she would be able to care for you during the times that James was at sea. It was just safer for you to be in her care and for her to believe I was gone for good or

James might see through my ruse. My old friend, Tim, smuggled me out of state and put me in touch with a distant relative and as soon as I'm able to find a job and save enough money, I'll come back for you as you are my beating heart. Please be brave.

Of course, she never did, and I hated her and hated the world I was born into for a very long time. It wasn't until I was married that I learned that she had died from a lung infection before she had an opportunity to return. To this day, I'm grateful that I had Helen's love to fall back on. She had kept the painting for me until I had made a home for myself and even then, I hid it away so I wouldn't have to explain it to anyone, especially my young daughter.

Kate is wearing her years well. In that she is like my Mary. But Kate looks more like my mother every day. And this morning before she left for Boston to see Ross, I realized that she has begun to appreciate the similarities to Brigid, in a good way. She's left the painting here with me while she's gone, says I've been parted from it for too long, but you can't miss what you don't remember. With any luck Dr. Ben's magic pills will do more than cause constipation and headaches, but will keep the door to the past open for a little while longer. I need time to say my proper goodbyes to those I've loved.

And Kate needs time to hear from me why she is the right woman to carry on Brigid's loving legacy. Maybe Kate's new relationship will give her a better perspective and just maybe she and I will close all the gaps together. I pray this medication keeps on working long enough for both of us. I would love to see what I've missed and especially the home where Helen kept our secrets.